Black Scarface 5

FEAR IS STRONGER THAN LOVE

Written By

JIMMY DASAINT

Copyright © 2025.
DaSaint Entertainment
All rights reserved.
ISBN:978-0-9992273-6-7

Dedication

xxx

Dedication

Dedicated to my mother, Charlotte Belinda Mathis, and my brother, Sean Mathis; may they both rest in peace.

Contents

CHAPTER 1		14
Philadelphia, PA, 5:45 P.M.		14
CHAPTER 2		19
Villanova, PA		19
CHAPTER 3		22
Abington PA		22
CHAPTER 4		26
Washington DC		26
CHAPTER 5		28
Chestnut Hill		28
CHAPTER 6		30
Downtown Philadelphia		30
CHAPTER 7		32
North Philadelphia		32
CHAPTER 8		34
West Philly		34
CHAPTER 9		36
Downtown Philadelphia		36
CHAPTER 10		38
Downtown Philadelphia		38
CHAPTER 11		40
CHAPTER 12		42
Downtown Philly		42
CHAPTER 13		44
Northeast Philly		44
CHAPTER 14		46
Chevy Chase, Maryland		46

CHAPTER 15	48
Chestnut Hill, Philadelphia	48
CHAPTER 16	52
Washington DC	52
CHAPTER 17	54
Downtown Philadelphia	54
CHAPTER 18	56
Ardmore, PA	56
CHAPTER 19	59
South Philadelphia	59
CHAPTER 20	61
Eastern Pennsylvania	61
CHAPTER 21	63
Bethesda Maryland	63
CHAPTER 22	65
Island of Antigua	65
CHAPTER 23	67
The Ritz-Carlton Hotel	67
CHAPTER 24	69
CHAPTER 25	71
CHAPTER 26	75
Chestnut Hill, Philadelphia	75
CHAPTER 27	77
CHAPTER 28	81
Fairmount Park, Philadelphia	81
CHAPTER 29	85
Chinatown	85
CHAPTER 30	87
Northeast Philadelphia	87

CHAPTER 31	89
Santa Marta, Colombia	89
CHAPTER 32	91
Northeast Philly	91
CHAPTER 33	93
Chinatown	93
CHAPTER 34	96
140 S. Broad Street, Philadelphia	96
CHAPTER 35	98
CHAPTER 36	100
Manayunk Philadelphia	100
CHAPTER 37	103
CHAPTER 38	105
Philadelphia	105
CHAPTER 39	107
CHAPTER 40	109
Atlantic City, NJ	109
CHAPTER 41	111
Chinatown	111
CHAPTER 42	114
CHAPTER 43	116
Center City	116
CHAPTER 44	118
Chapter 45	120
Upper Darby, PA	120
CHAPTER 46	122
CHAPTER 47	124
CHAPTER 48	126
Temple Hospital	126
CHAPTER 49	128
CHAPTER 50	131
Washington, D.C	131

CHAPTER 51	135
Montgomery County	135
CHAPTER 52	137
Downtown Philly	137
CHAPTER 53	139
North Philadelphia	139
CHAPTER 54	141
Ardmore, PA	141
CHAPTER 55	143
Northeast Philadelphia	143
CHAPTER 56	146
CHAPTER 57	149
Ardmore, Pa	149
CHAPTER 58	152
Laurel Hill Cemetery	152
CHAPTER 59	154
Downtown Philadelphia	154
CHAPTER 60	156
Downtown Philly	156
CHAPTER 61	158
CHAPTER 62	163
West Philadelphia	163
CHAPTER 63	165
West Philly	165
CHAPTER 64	167
Laurel Hill Cemetery	167
CHAPTER 65	169
West Philly	169
CHAPTER 66	179
Washington, DC, The White House	179
EPILOGUE	181

Part One

"Mastering others is strength. Mastering yourself is true power." - LAO TZU.

CHAPTER 1

Philadelphia, PA, 5:45 P.M.

In his large, opulent office, located on the top floor of his newly renovated building, Face sat at his desk reading over real estate reports. For ten years, Face studied the real estate game and became a major player in the Philly and South Jersey real estate communities. He was also the second-highest owner-investor of Commercial and Residential real estate property in Philadelphia.

Face placed the reports inside the top drawer of his desk and stood up from his chair. Then he walked over to his large glass window and stared out at the city.

Memories from his past life began to cloud his mind. He thought about his beginnings and where it all started. Being raised by a single black mother was hard at times, but those tough times groomed him to become the man he is today. Suddenly, a single tear rolled down his face. The thought of his best friend, Reese, would always get the best of him. Reese's death had always been a hard pill to swallow.

Many times, they had talked about one day running the world together. Being former drug dealers, they made it successfully out of the heartless drug game, but those dreams faded away with Reese's death. As Face stood there in deep thought, the tap on the door woke him from his daze. After wiping his tear away, he said, "Come in, Janet."

In walked a beautiful black young woman with an hourglass figure and dreamy hazel eyes that accentuated her caramel complexion. Her name was Janet Debose, and she had been his personal secretary for three years. Face had hired her straight out of Temple University. When it came to business, Janet was one of a kind. "Mr. Smith, you have a visitor," she told him.

"What I tell you about that?" he smirked.

"I mean, Face, you have a visitor out in the lobby", she replied.

"Who is it?"

"Mark Livingston," she said with a devilish smirk.

After a long pause, Face said, "Okay, send him in."

Face sat down at his desk and patiently waited. Then in walked a tall, white man with piercing blue eyes and an athlete build. He stood around 6 foot 3 inches with short, dark, curly hair. Mark Livingston was a 43-year-old bachelor and one of the richest men in America. His estimated net worth was around four billion dollars. Not only was he wealthy beyond words, but he was very well connected in both the real estate and political worlds. From New York to Washington D.C., there was no one he couldn't reach or wouldn't answer his phone call... no one except Face.

"Have a seat, Mark."

They shook hands, and Face politely asked, "So, how can I help you?"

"I called you four times this week, and I can't ever get you on the phone. Every time I try, Janet tells me that you're busy or in an important meeting."

"Well, it's true, but you're here now, so how can I help you?"

Mark looked Face straight into his eyes, "Are you ready to sell? My offer still stands."

Face smiled and said, "And my answer is still the same. I'm never selling my entire real estate portfolio to you or anyone else. Just like your wealthy father left you a ton of money for generational wealth, just like you and your wealthy friends. The Waltons, Koch, Mellons, and Rockefellers. So, like I told you before, Mark, I'm one black man that you can't buy or control."

"A billion dollars is more than enough, and you and I both know it. I can have the funds wired to you in 20 minutes or less."

"Keep your money; I'm not interested in selling my soul to another blue-eyed devil," Face said with authority. "So the answer is still no!"

Mark stood up from his chair, fuming. He wasn't used to being turned down or offended by anyone. For five years, he had been trying to buy Face out, but Face would always refuse his offers. "You black son of a bitch! I know who you are! I know everything there is about you. You're nothing but a low-down dirty scum bag drug dealer that made all your money from taking from others."

"Just like your father!" Face replied with a smile on his face.

"You leave my father's name out of your mouth!"

"Like I said, you're nothing but the scum of the earth, and your time will come. Trust me, your crown will fall off, and I'll be there laughing when it does."

"Just make sure yours doesn't fall off first," Face said.

"We'll see about that. Enjoy your day, Face!" Mark said before he stormed out of the office and slammed the door behind himself.

Face didn't take Mark's threats too kindly. In another place and time, he would have Mark buried in a cement grave.

In all of his years, he had never met anyone like Mark Livingston. He was a man of great wealth and power who had inherited a real estate fortune from his father, Sam Livingston. Face had known everything there was about the Livingston family. A father who had made hundreds of millions from the Stock Market and his spoiled Harvard dropout son who had everything given to him. Mark was Sam and Margaret Livingston's only child. He grew up in the Suburbs of Philadelphia, where his parents had still lived. Mark was a wealthy playboy who lived and played by his own rules. He was consumed by wealth, power, sex, and greed.

Two years earlier, Face had his private investigator find out everything there was about Mark Livingston. They were two men of unlimited power who despised each other. One grew up privileged, and the other came from nothing. Each one had something to prove.

Face stood up from his chair and looked out the window. He watched as Mark got into his black Tesla and sped off down the street.

Janet tapped on the door and peeped inside, "Are you okay, Face?"

"I'm fine, Janet, but I need you to get Quincy on the line and tell him to meet me at my home."

"I'm on it now," she said before leaving out the door.

"You want war motherfucker, then you can have it any way you want it," Face said to himself.

CHAPTER 2

Villanova, PA

Inside his beautiful twelve-room mansion, Mark Livingston sat at the large round glass table, surrounded by three of his closest friends and business partners: Carter Samuels, his 58-year-old high-powered lawyer; Leo Renolds, the 42-year-old U.S. Attorney General, and Sergio Miller, a professional hit man that he had on his payroll.

As Mark sipped on a glass of white wine, the three men all sat in silence. "I called all of y'all here to talk about a major problem I have. And I'm gonna need all of y'all to help me get rid of it," Mark said.

"What is it? Or who is it?" Leo asked with curiosity.

"It's that no good son of a bitch Norman Smith Jr. Or the man better known as Face. He has been a major thorn in my side for a while now, and I want him gone," Mark replied.

Shock expressions were plastered on each of their faces. They all knew who Face was. He was infamous all throughout the Philadelphia Tri-State. Men feared him, and women craved him, but everyone respected him.

"Face is your problem?" Sergio asked. "He's major!"

"I don't give a damn what or who he is, this city is mine, and I'm going to control it all, and Face has to be eliminated," Mark shouted as he continued to drink his glass of wine.

"Once upon a time, he was a street legend, and I heard he is the man responsible for the death of Senator C.W Watson and countless others," Leo said.

"Don't believe all those rumors, Leo; this guy is not the man y'all think he is. No man has a power like that, and if so, it's about to come to an end because this time Face has met his match."

Mark looked at the faces of all the men; he could sense fear inside the room, but it didn't sit well. "All y'all with me or not?" Each of the men nodded their heads in agreement.

"Well, good, because in the next six months, I'm going to do everything in my power to ruin that man! He is going to wish he never heard the name Mark Livingston."

"Let's do it", Leo said. "He's had a run way too long, and it's time to get him out of here. Either by force, illegal or legal, but Face must go."

Mark smiled and shook his head. "I want his company! I want to destroy everything he loves, and I want him out of Philadelphia!"

"I'm on it now, Mark; I have to start making some phone calls. We will need a big hook to catch a big fish", Sergio said before he shook everyone's hand and walked out of the room.

"I'll have my private investigator Ken start watching him, and I'll get some people that I work with to start checking out all his company records," Leo said.

"I'll call you in a few days to let you know what's found," he said before shaking hands and walking out of the room. "Carter, you've been very quiet. Is something wrong?" Mark asked. Carter approached Mark with a serious look on his face. "Can I be totally honest with you?"

"Yes, what is it?" Mark asked.

"I don't think you should let jealousy and greed control you."

"It's not jealousy or greed, my friend. It's power, and I want it all," Mark Livingston said with a smirk.

CHAPTER 3

Abington PA

Standing outside of his large gated six-bedroom home, Face walked over and sat down on the hood of his black Maybach truck. Suddenly, one by one, a line of luxury cars began to enter the gate. A Porsche, BMW, Range Rover, and Mercedes all parked beside each other. When the doors had opened, out came four of Face's closest friends and confidantes. Quincy, his longtime friend and hitman. King, his cousin to whom he had passed the drug game torch. Frank Underworld "Simms," the C.E.O. of one of the biggest records labels in America. And his loyal and trusted street general, Simon "Black Gotti" Carter, one of the biggest and most violent drug kingpins on the East Coast.

The men all followed Face into the house and walked into a large, private conference room. Sitting down at a round conference table was a short young black man. He was typing something on his laptop. Each of the men sat down, facing a large T.V. monitor. "I'm glad that y'all was able to make it. I wouldn't have reached out if the matter was not important, but I'm sorry to say it is!" Face said to the group of men. "This is my computer tech, Marvin. He is one of the best hackers, technicians, and cyber analysts in the country. Two years ago, Marvin graduated from M.I.T., and since then, he has been working for me."

"So Marvin is good?" King asked.

"No, Marvin is great!" Face replied.

"So what's going on? I received an emergency text and came straight over", Black Gotti said.

"Marvin, can you bring up the photos?" Face said.

The faces of four men appeared on the large monitor. As everyone stared up at the screen, Marvin began talking. "The man on the top right is Mark Livingston. He is one of the wealthiest men in America. Net worth 4.6 billion dollars. He is a single playboy with over a dozen beautiful women he can call on any given day or night.

The older man on the top left is Carter Samuels, one of the top lawyers and partners at the Samuel-Klein and Linden Law offices. He graduated from the University of Penn in 1989 and then finished up at the Wharton School of Business. He has been married to his wife, Sheila, for 32 years, and they have two daughters. On the bottom right is Leo Renolds; he is currently the United States Attorney General, and he and Mark are best friends. They met each other at Harvard University and have remained close ever since. Leo is married to Elizabeth Renolds, and they have two children, a son and a daughter. Leo has a spotless record, and he was personally appointed by the President of the United States. The word in Washington, DC, is that Leo will be next in line to take over the F.B.I. He is very well-connected and respected in the political sphere. Last but not least, the man on the bottom left is Sergio Miller, one of the best-hired mercenaries and hitmen on the planet. With over 200 kills all across the globe. I'm talking about Siberia, Iran, South Africa, South America, and all across the states. His nickname is the hand of Satan, and there is nothing he wouldn't do for Mark Livingston. Everyone that Mark Livingston had ever had a problem with had suddenly disappeared, and not only that but somehow, Mr. Livingston managed to purchase full control of their companies. I believe that Sergio is the man responsible for the disappearances and death of all Mark's enemies."

Face stood up and looked around the table. "This man has been trying to buy my company for years. Each time, I turned him down, but he kept coming with more offers. Earlier today, he came to my office and threatened to take me and my company down. It was a threat I didn't take lightly. Over the years, I called on y'all many times, but this is different. These four men are surrounded by power and unlimited wealth, and they want everything that I built.

They want to destroy me and will do anything to see my demise. Right now, I have a private eye finding out all he can on each of them. With Mark's political power and influence, he can sabotage and destroy everything we have built over the last 20 years. I'm sure they are researching all of you now to find out who I'm connected to. They have the resources and power to make each of our lives miserable. So today, I ask that we join up and fight this new enemy. An enemy like none we have faced before. Because there is nothing worse than a man who has the world in his hand but is still not satisfied.! A man with unlimited wealth and power who won't stop until he has more!"

Quincy stood up and said, "Count me in!"

King stood up and said, "Count me in as well."

Black Gotti and Underworld both stood up at the same time. "Whatever you need, Face I'm here," Underworld said.

"You already know, Face, without question, I'm here for you." Black Gotti said.

Face smiled and nodded his head. "Good. Well, I sent the wife and kids away to our vacation home in the Caribbean while I handled my business, and I think y'all should do the same. This guy, Mark, plays dirty, so we must all be cautious and on top alert. Marvin will reach out to y'all on a new cryptic messenger that each of you will be given the password to. Each message will automatically delete after thirty minutes."

After everyone had left, Face walked outside to his beautiful large backyard. Sitting beside him were his two large rottweilers, Michael Angelo and Gabriel, named after the two Arch Angels that sat on the side of God. Face looked up at the sky and said a silent prayer to himself. After a long, deep breath, he turned and walked back into his home with Michael Angelo, and Gabriel right beside him.

CHAPTER 4

Washington DC

One week later...

Mark Livingston walked down the long marble hallway and approached a beautiful white woman sitting down at a desk. "Good to see you again, Amber," he said with a big smile on his face.

"You as well, Mark, the Attorney General is expecting you," she said, blushing.

Mark leaned down and placed his lips to her ear. "I'm in town til the morning. I'll be at the condo around 10 P.M. Make sure you come over with that black outfit I brought you."

"Can I bring my friend again?" she asked.

"Yeah, why not? That was fun last time," he said with a smile before he walked into Leo Renolds' office.

Sitting down at his large black desk, Leo was holding an envelope in his hand. "You got something?" Mark said as he sat down in the chair.

Leo passed Mark the envelope and said, "Yes, we have a lot on Face and his closest friends."

Mark sat back and opened the envelope. As he began to read through it, his eyes lit up with excitement. "So these are all the members of his inner circle, huh?"

"Yes, they are all the people Face has been associated with over the past twenty years," Leo replied.

"Frank Underworld, Simms, Simon "Black Gotti" Carter, and Darious "King" Smith. Wow, what a cast of characters", Mark laughed.

"They definitely are, but to be totally honest, they are all major players in the drug game and very well connected all over the country. Frank is respected throughout the music and film industry. King and Gotti are major both up and down the East Coast. My sources told me that Face is the boss of bosses and still the biggest drug boss in the United States. He uses his real estate company, which he built with his wife, as a front", Leo said.

"Can you prove it?"

"They all run a tight ship, and it's been virtually impossible to break any of their inner circles. So far, wiretaps and surveillance haven't gotten us anything, but I won't stop until I get something on one of them", Leo said with a serious face.

CHAPTER 5

Chestnut Hill

A large group of F.B.I. and D.E.A. agents swarmed onto Face's property. With a search warrant in hand, they looked all over the home for anything that could be used as evidence to bring Face down. With a calm look on his Face, Face stood there smoking a Cuban cigar. His two rottweilers were seated beside him. After an hour of searching the property, the lead agent approached Face and said, "We confiscated a few computers; you'll be contacted soon by someone from the F.B.I. office."

"Don't worry; my lawyer will be reaching out soon. We both know that this was an illegal search." Face replied.

"Hey, I'm just doing my job," the agent said before he turned and walked away.

After all the agents had left, Face called his home security team to come by the house and check for any bugs placed by the F.B.I. He wasn't worried about them finding anything because he didn't do any of his personal business at his Chestnut Hill home. Face understood the game and how the rich played it. They would use wealth, power, and influence to get things done. Only someone with great power could have the F.B.I. raid one of his homes. With a calm look on his face deep down, Face was livid. He knew this was a game of chess and not checkers. Only one King would survive, and he was determined to be that one. Face took out his secured cell phone and called Quincy.

"I want you to reach out to someone and see if we can turn them. Maybe it will all work, maybe not, but we both know that the enemy of my enemy is a friend. I'll text you all the info shortly."

"Okay, Face, I'm on it," Quincy said before the line went dead.

CHAPTER 6

Downtown Philadelphia

Mark and his lawyer, Carter Samuels, were seated in a large conference room discussing the day's events. "How did it go?"

"The raid was completed about an hour ago. Over 25 agents were at the Chestnut Hill property. I'm sure it was very uncomfortable for Face," Carter said.

"Good! I want him to feel uncomfortable. Was his wife and children at home?"

"No, Face was there alone."

"Well, I want him and all the members of his crew to feel uncomfortable and to know that it is not a game. Who's next?"

"His cousin King. The FBI already has search warrants signed by a judge to raid his property as well. Then they will get all the others," Carter smirked.

"Good job! Make sure you send Leo a bonus."

"It's already been sent to Leo's offshore account in the Cayman Islands."

"Hopefully, he will get tired of all the harassment and sell out like everyone else has done. The pressure can become very overwhelming for people. Look what it did to Theodore. It broke him, and he decided to sell me everything. How is Theodore Roberts doing these days?" Carter started typing into his laptop.

"A year ago, his wife divorced him and left with the two kids. He lost his three-million-dollar home in Maryland and his vacation home in Hawaii. He's been sued by former employees, and now he's completely bankrupt. Those raids on his properties destroyed him. Once they found all the illegal evidence that had been planted, it was over for Theodore. He had no other option but to sell his real estate company to you. The fines and penalties were just too much for him to escape. Then, once he was threatened with federal prison times, it was over for sure."

"He's lucky that I got Leo to get rid of the indictment, or else he would be serving his seven years in prison. All he had to do was sell the first time I asked, and all that would have been avoided. I want Face to feel the same pain that Theodore felt."

"Don't worry, he will," Carter laughed.

CHAPTER 7

North Philadelphia

A few days later...

"The Feds raided everyone's home! Luckily, they were all prepared and on point," Quincy said. "But there were a lot of drugs confiscated on the streets. In Philly, King lost a hundred kilos, and Gotti lost forty. A few of their top lieutenants were arrested, but their bails were paid, and they're back out. The FBI and DEA are all over Philly, making it hard for anyone to get money," Quincy added. "Just make sure they get the best lawyers and tell everyone to shut down all drug operations at least until this situation is over and dealt with. It's going to be hard going against a billionaire and the US Attorney General, but nothing is impossible, and no one is invincible. We have gone up against powerful men before and look what happened. It might take some time, but the game of chess is not about speed but about patience, which is the one that makes the first mistake. Did you reach out to your friend?"

"Yes, he's afraid, but I believe he'll come around soon. Revenge is a powerful tool to walk away from."

"You're right, but fear is stronger than revenge! We have to make him feel safe and know that everyone has a weakness, even Mark Livingston," Face said.

"I'll stay on him."

"Good, and do whatever it takes to get him on board, he'll be an asset."

As Quincy walked out of the house, in walked King.

"This is some bullshit, cuz! The Feds is all over the city. I lost a whole shipment and so did Gotti."

"I know, and that's why I want everyone to shut down for a while. "

"That will cause a major drought. No drugs on the streets will cause chaos. The murder rate will get sky-high. What will I tell the Colombians?" King said.

"Don't worry, I'll handle it, and I'll speak to the Cartel leaders. They will understand and know that it's better to be safe than sorry."

"You gotta fix this shit, Face! You need to find a way to erase this nigga Mark or else..."

"Or else what?" Face asked.

"Or else he is going to erase us!" King answered before he angrily stormed out of the house.

CHAPTER 8

West Philly

7:30 A.M...

Early the next morning, Face had Quincy pick him up, and together, they headed to see an old friend from the neighborhood. When they reached Doc's house, some old memories instantly came back. They had both known Doc ever since they were teenage boys, running around the neighborhood selling drugs and robbing people. Doc was like no other. He was the only white man in the hood, and no one paid him any mind. He was loved by all, but only a few knew of his past and deepest secrets.

Doc was a sociopathic, homosexual serial killer who would torture and then eat each of his victims. He was a man possessed with a dark spirit. The only person he respected and considered a real friend was Face. For him, there was nothing Doc wouldn't do. Nothing. Inside Doc's basement was a large hospital gurney with straps all around it. There were three large color monitors, an automated external defibrillator, and other surgical tools scattered around on different shelves. In the corner was a small desk with an Apple iMac computer on top of it.

In the opposite corner of the basement, Face and Quincy stood in total shock. Chained to a concrete wall was a tall, naked blonde-haired man with large breasts and a vagina. "Oh, don't y'all worry about Anabella; he's my wife," Doc said as he continued on without a care in the world. "Face, how can I help you this time? It's been a few years since we worked together. I really enjoyed working with you, Face."

"I'm going to need your help soon. I have a serious problem. I'm trying to eliminate," Face answered.

"Is he handsome? I'm looking for a new wife to join my stable. Annabelle needs a friend," Doc smirked.

"I think you'll enjoy him, Doc. I just got to put my plan together and get him to you."

"Well, if you need me for anything, I have no problem helping you."

"Thanks, Doc. Enjoy your day," Face said as he and Quincy walked up the stairs.

"That dude is crazy!" Quincy whispered.

"Crazy ain't the word. Doc is a maniac, but we both know he can be trusted and counted on, and his loyalty is unmatched," Face replied.

CHAPTER 9

Downtown Philadelphia

Underworld Entertainment...

10:24 A.M.

Frank "Underworld" Simms stood around with a frustrated look on his face. He watched as a group of IRS agents ransacked his office, confiscating computers, files, and boxes of music material. A short, white, heavyset man walked up to Frank and said, "Mr. Simms, we will be back in a few days, and you can expect a full audit."

"This is some bullshit, and you know it!"

"I'm just doing my job, sir; take it up with my bosses at the agency."

Frank watched as the agents walked out of the office carrying large boxes. As soon as they left, he called Face on a secured cellphone line. "Wassup, Frank? The IRS just left my office! They ransacked my whole building, Face! Now they talking about doing an audit this week," Frank yelled.

"Calm down, Frank! What do you have to worry about? Your record company is legit. All your paperwork is legit. Get your lawyers on the phone and tell them to do their job. You pay them enough! Your money is accountable. You have the biggest female singer on the planet, Ashley Jay. Didn't she sell over 50 million albums last year? Let the Feds do an audit, they won't find shit!" Face said into the phone.

"You're right, Face; I'm just not used to this. Being watched by the FBI, IRS, audits, harassment by the Feds. It's nerve-wracking."

"Don't worry, Frank, I'm on it. Trust me, my friend, I'm on it!"

"I believe you, Face; you have always been a man of your word. I won't start doubting you now. I'll keep you posted on everything", Frank said as he walked onto the elevator.

"I might need a big favor from you, Frank."

"Anything, just let me know."

"Well, I might need your artist, Ashley Jay."

"Just let me know when and where, and it's done. I'll call you in a few days after the IRS do their audit."

"Okay, fine. And remember Frank, every bully eventually finds their match."

CHAPTER 10

Downtown Philadelphia

Rittenhouse Claridge…

Inside his luxury condominium penthouse, Mark sat back on the king-size bed, watching as two beautiful exotic women were making love to each other. Sipping on a bottle of Armand de Brignac Gold Champagne. Mark was completely turned on. Since his teenage years, Mark had always been a lady's man-playboy who enjoyed the comfort and sexual satisfaction of different women. His preferences were tall, slim blondes and busty brunettes. He had personally bedded over a thousand women. Models, actresses, singers, athletes, and a few reality TV stars had all been added to Mark's list of sex partners.

"I want you to finish eating her ass!" Mark told the Asian beauty.

"Okay, Daddy."

Mark sat back, gulping the champagne down his throat while rubbing on his erect dick.

"Okay, Brandi, it's your turn," he said to the tall, gorgeous blonde. After the women finished pleasing each other, Mark joined in on the threesome. He was a handsome playboy billionaire enjoying his best life.

Germantown Philadelphia...

Inside his black Mercedes Benz SUV, Gotti watched through the rear-view mirror as the red and blue lights flashed behind his cars. Gotti pulled over to the side of the road and watched as the two FBI agents got out of the tinted black unmarked car and approached his vehicle. "How can I help y'all?"

"License and registration, Mr. Carter," one of the agents said in an aggressive tone.

"This is some bullshit, and y'all know it," Gotti said as he passed the agent his license and registration.

In total frustration, Gotti sat back in total silence. He was livid, but at that moment, there wasn't anything he could do about it.

"Face, you gotta fix this shit," Gotti whispered to himself.

Thirty minutes later, Gotti was still sitting inside his car waiting.

CHAPTER 11

Two days later.

Ken Nelson was Mark's private investigator. For the past year Ken had been paid to dig up dirt on all of Mark's enemies. He had gathered dirt on Politicians, Athletes, Ex-lovers, business partners, and so many more. Ken was a short, stocky white man who wore glasses. He looked like a high school science teacher that had all the answers to any question. He was very meticulous with his job and took it seriously.

Inside his parked car, across the street from Face's real estate building, Ken typed into a small laptop and the description of everyone that came and left the building. As he took down his notes, he had no idea that a set of eyes was watching his every move. Parked two cars behind Ken's car was Quincy. Just like Ken had been watching and taking notes for Mark, Quincy had been doing the same for Face. Quincy knew everything there was to know about Ken Nelson. In the art of war, information on your enemy was the key to your success. Quincy knew the game all too well. For years, Quincy had been the protective shadow behind Face. Lurking in the shadows of all their enemies.

"Hello?" Face said, answering his burner cellphone.

"I'm hearing a lot of things coming out of Philly. None of it is good," a voice said.

"It's been bad, but trust me, I'm on it."

"I know you are my good friend. We have been through way worse than this." the man said in a Spanish accent.

"I'm going to need those shipments to be held up until I fix this problem," King said.

"Will all your men be okay with that?"

"Yes, I talked to them all. Philly is hot right now. The FBI, DEA, and IRS are all over the place. It's been a hectic week, but so far, no major arrest or seizure of product. I just want to be cautious."

"Okay, just take your time, my friend. If you need me, I'm on the first red-eye leaving Columbia."

"Thanks, brother; talk to you soon," Face said before ending the call.

CHAPTER 12

Downtown Philly

Mark and his high-priced Lawyer, Carter Samuels, were seated inside Mark's downtown office. "We just acquired twenty-five new commercial properties and ten residential properties from South Jersey," Carter said, passing Mark a thin black folder.

"Just sign off for me, Carter. You're authorized to sign my name on all legal documents, so just do it," Mark said, passing the folder back. "What's wrong?"

"Nothing, I'm fine, just don't understand how the FBI, DEA, and IRS raids didn't find anything on Face and his crew. It's like they knew the Feds were coming, and they were prepared and ready. This guy, Face, is really getting on my nerves, Carter!"

"Did you talk to Sergio?"

"I did. He's on it. He said he even got one of his best men headed down to the Caribbean," Mark said with a devilish smirk.

"That should scare Face, and maybe he will see that he can't win this war," Carter said.

"First of all, his money ain't long enough. I'll spend every penny if I have to destroy this man. I want him gone! I want everything he has!" Mark stood up and said.

"Well, Leo is doing whatever you ask of him. Sergio is waiting for the right moment, and opportunity to put a bullet in his head, and Ken is out gathering all the necessary information for us to make sure nothing leads back to any of us. Just stay patient, my friend. Face is on borrowed time," Carter replied.

"You're right, Carter. I'll talk to you later. Right now, I have two beautiful women waiting for me at the Penthouse."

"Wow, I'm surprised you're still entertaining them," Carter said.

"I'm not! I have two new girls. A black and Spanish this time." Mark smiled as they walked out of the office.

"Don't you ever get tired and need some rest?"

"I'll rest when I die," Mark replied. "And I don't plan on dying no time soon."

CHAPTER 13

Northeast Philly

At just 23 years old, Marvin was considered a genius, with an IQ of 130. He was one of the best computer technicians and internet hackers on the East Coast. He had graduated from MIT with honors. There was no computer system he couldn't hack into. After graduating college, he had over fifty high-paying job offers waiting for him. He turned them all down and chose to work for Face. The reason for that was that Marvin was the younger brother of Janet, Face's personal secretary. Marvin sat back, typing into his laptop. He had just ordered three new high-powered GPS tracking devices. Once he had them placed, he could watch someone's every move.

South Jersey...

Two-time Grammy award-winning singer Ashley Jay was lying back on a large sectional inside her lavish living room. Large picture frames and platinum plaques were hanging on the decorated walls. Right over her head was a large gold and silver chandelier that accentuated the light inside the room. Her entire home was opulent, surrounded by expensive antiques that she had purchased from all over the world.

At only twenty-nine years old, Ashley was living her best life. She knew what it was like to turn nothing into something. Born on the cold, heartless streets of Camden, NJ, she had known poverty firsthand. Through all the pain she had endured as a poor white child, from mental to physical abuse, it was her powerful voice that saved her. One day, after meeting and singing for Franks "Underworld" Simms, the CEO of Underworld Entertainment, her young life was forever changed. Laying back, sipping on a glass of white wine, Ashley reached for her ringing cellphone.

"Hey, Frank, is everything set for the BET awards?" she asked.

"Yes, it's all been taken care of. But I'm calling you for something else."

"Anything for you, Frank. I told you that I'm forever indebted to you."

"Well, I'll be over shortly to talk about it," Frank said.

"Well, I hear the concern in your voice. Don't you worry, I'm here for you always, and whatever you need me to do, consider it done", Ashley told him.

CHAPTER 14

Chevy Chase, Maryland

Located just outside of Washington, DC...

Looking through the scope of his Remington M24 sniper rifle, Sergio had the crosshairs locked on his target. After taking a long, deep breath, his finger softly pulled the trigger. In an instant, the armor-piercing bullet entered and exploded into the man's head, killing him instantly. Hiding behind a tree in a wooded area, Sergio watched as the man's two bodyguards were in complete shock. They quickly ran for cover, saving their own lives. Looking over at their boss, they couldn't help but see his splattered brain matter all over the ground. After packing up his rifle, Sergio ran through the woods dressed in camouflage from head to toe. After the job was done, Sergio took out his cell phone and called Mark.

"It's done! Got him leaving the golf course," he said.

"Good job! Another enemy I can cross off my list. Now I'm sure his wife will sell the company to me. I'll have Carter transfer your funds into your private account in an hour. Any word yet on your friend?"

"He will be arriving in Antigua in the morning."

"Can you trust him?" Mark asked.

"Yes, he's my best man for the job. Everything will be taken care of, sir," Sergio assured him.

"Okay, fine, I'll talk to you when you get back. Right now, I'm in the middle of two beautiful women," Mark said before ending the call.

After changing out of his gear, Sergio got back into his black-tinted Ford pickup and headed down the road. He was a heartless killer who had no emotion or sympathy for others. He considered most wealthy men weak and got a privilege out of killing them. His only friends were the dead presidents on dollar bills and his large collection of guns. Sergio's ultimate goal was to kill Face. To be the man that took his life would be his biggest prize. The thought of having Face in his crosshairs made his dick hard.

CHAPTER 15

Chestnut Hill, Philadelphia

Early the next day...

Sitting at a private booth at the Iron Hill Grille restaurant.

"I'm going to need an Ambulance, new guns, a bulletproof vest, and for you to contact Jerome down at the Cemetery," Face told Quincy.

"Don't worry, I'm on it, Face. I'll call Jerome as soon as I leave. Anything new?" Quincy asked.

"The Feds is auditing Frank's company records, he's pissed about that, but Frank knows the deal. We talked a few days ago," Face replied.

"What about King, Gotti, and all the others?"

"They'll all be fine; I reassured them that everything will be back in order. Plus, I talked to the Cartel; they understand what's happening," Face said as he sipped on a glass of red wine.

"How's the wife and kids?"

"They're good. Being down in the Caribbean was good for them. Just until all of this blows over," Face said.

"I'm afraid to ask, but how is Doc?"

"Doc is Doc! He's a man that's happy inside his own world. As long as he's on our side, I'm satisfied. He's been down with us for years. I'm not going to act like some of his tactics don't disturb me, but he's loyal to the team, and loyalty is mandatory in our line of business," Face replied.

"Marvin?"

"He's working on a few things for me right now. I told him to get us a few GPS trackers and to work on hacking into a few government accounts."

Quincy smiled and said, "That boy is a genius; I'm sure he'll find a way to break into any system we need him to."

"Did you hear about the Investment banker who was assassinated right outside the golf course?"

"I did, why wassup?"

"His name was Taylor Mitchell, and he used to work with Mark. Taylor owns a few lucrative beach properties all over Florida. They said the hit looked professional, and he had been receiving threats for months," Face said.

"What does this have to do with us?"

"I'm sure Mark had Sergio do the hit. It's his MO. We just need to stay on point, Quincy."

"Trust me, Face; I stay on point and in the shadows. I know how these people work and all the things they do to destroy and conquer."

Quincy looked over at Face and saw a concerned look on his face. In all the years they had worked together, he could count on one hand how many times he had seen that look on his friend.

"We've been through many battles together, Face. And we have won them all. This is just another obstacle that's in our way, and no obstacle is too big to overcome," Quincy said, placing his hand on Face's shoulder. "The bigger they are, the harder they fall," he added.

"Your cousin is going to be just fine," Queen said to her husband King.

"I hope so because I have never seen Face this uncomfortable in all my life," King replied.

"Did you ever think that maybe he's putting a master plan together? We are talking about Face, the biggest and baddest to ever do it," Queen said as she stepped out of the shower.

King walked out behind her and wrapped his arms around her waist. Then he began to softly kiss on the small of Queen's neck. "I'm sure he's up to something. He's a legend for a reason. It's because of him that we live in this six-bedroom home, far away from the dramas in the city. Face plays chess like a grandmaster while everyone else is playing checkers."

Queen turned around and looked deep into King's dark brown eyes. "Okay, bae, that's enough about Face. Whenever he needs you, I'm sure you'll be there, but right now, I'm standing here butt naked, and I need some dick right now," Queen said as she turned back around and bent over, showing her wide fat ass. Without hesitation, King slid his hard dick into the deepness of her paradise. Instantly, her loud moans filled up the bathroom. "Yes, daddy! Yes! Fuck me harder, daddy!" Queen moaned out as a powerful orgasm swept throughout her body.

CHAPTER 16

Washington DC

Inside the office of the U.S. Attorney General, a group of high government officials sat around talking. Sitting behind his desk, Leo asked, "So, men, how did the raids go?"

"So far, so good for the FBI," a man said.

"Right now, I have one of my top men currently auditing Frank Simms and his company, Underworld Entertainment," another man added.

"My men at the DEA are planning on a few more raids in every section of Philadelphia. We picked up a few small fries, but not major or of any significance," a tall white man said.

"So, Leo, what's all this about? Why are you adamant about this?" A short, bearded white man asked.

"Do y'all remember Norman Smith Jr., also known as Face?" Leo asked the men.

"Yes, how can we not! He beat the government in one of the biggest drug cases in U.S. History. His name has been connected to the murders of some very powerful men, but there has never been any proof or witnesses. Why do you ask?" One of the men said.

"Well, I have some very good sources that believe Face is still involved in the drug game," Leo replied.

"Isn't he into real estate now? His company is one of the biggest on the East Coast. Why would he jeopardize all of that to still be involved in the drug trade?" The tall white man asked with a bemused look on his face.

"Are you sure your sources are correct?" he added.

"I'm sure, and that's why I asked for the raids to take place in Philly. Face might not be the man selling the drugs, but my sources tell me that he has put some powerful drug lords in place to do his dirt for him," Leo shouted.

"If this is true, this could be big. He made us all look bad at his trial. I still don't know how he pulled it off," the short white man said.

"Do I have all y'all cooperation on this matter?" Leo asked.

All the men inside the room nodded in agreement. Each one of them knew how a case of this magnitude would help their careers.

CHAPTER 17

Downtown Philadelphia

While Face was away from the office, he depended on Janet to run the day-to-day business. She was so much more than just a secretary. Janet Debose was an important piece of Face's circle. She was responsible for keeping everyone in order. Running the social media accounts, paying the bills, setting up all the important meetings, and so much more. Janet was someone Face trusted and could count on. "Jefferey, are all the accounts done?"

"Yes, ma'am," a young man answered as he typed into his laptop.

"Mary, have you finished payroll for this week?"

"I'll be done in an hour," a woman replied.

Janet smiled and headed towards her office. When she sat down at her desk, she took out the burner cell phone that Face had given her and called Face.

"Wassup, Janet?" Face answered.

"Just checking in. Everything down here is running smoothly. I got the team working extra hard," she said.

"Okay, fine, please make sure you have security with you when you come and go and always..."

"Watch my surroundings," Janet interrupted.

"Exactly. Things are getting crazy out here, and I wouldn't want anything to happen to you."

"I'll be fine, Face. How are Tasha and the kids?"

"They're doing fine. Thanks for booking their trip and getting them out of the country."

"Anything for you, Face. Thank you for giving my little brother Marvin a job. He's very excited about working with you," Janet said.

"He's a very talented young man. I have big plans for Marvin."

"Well, thank you. I'm about to go back and check on the team. I'll touch back in a few hours," Janet said before ending the call.

CHAPTER 18

Ardmore, PA

Inside their six-bedroom lavish home, situated on two acres of pristine land, Sam and Margaret Livingston were living a life of peace and tranquility. Their son Mark had purchased the multi-million-dollar home for his parents' 50th Anniversary. As they sat back by the pool, enjoying the burning hot sun, Mark walked outside to join them.

"Mom, Dad, how is everything going today?"

"Today has been wonderful, son. We've just been relaxing and enjoying this nice weather," Margaret said as she sipped on a cold glass of lemonade.

"Is everything okay with you, Mark?" his father asked.

"Yes, couldn't be any better. I just acquired a few new lucrative properties that are down in Florida. And soon, I'll be buying a business that I've been trying to purchase for some time now, " Mark replied.

"Just remember what I taught you, Mark, to never settle for second. If you want something, then go out and get it and let nothing or no one stand in your way," Sam said.

"You're a Livingston, and we don't accept second or failure," Margaret added.

Mark smiled and nodded his head in agreement. His parents had meant the world to him. Since he was a child, they had instilled in him the meaning of power and wealth. Once a week, Mark would come over to just relax and enjoy his parents' company. They would constantly remind him of who he was. A Livingston. From a long line of wealthy men and women. The Livingston bloodline traced back to a former Vice President, a General from the Civil War, and even the founder of the Ku Klux Klan. Mark was a part of the new generation, a man of great power and wealth, but he was also consumed by greed, hate, and destruction.

"There's a meeting later tonight down at the lodge. Many of your closest friends will be there," Sam said as they all got up and walked into the house.

"I know, and I wouldn't miss it for the world. I'll bring Carter, Sergio, and Ken along. I'll also see if Leo is available," Mark replied.

"Yeah, you do that because Leo missed the last few meetings," Sam said as he sat down on the sofa.

"Leo's a very important man, Father. Running things in D.C. takes a lot of hard work," Mark said as he sat down beside his parents.

"Just know that I'm very proud of you, son, and all of your friends. We need more good men like y'all to help keep the peasants down and where they belong," Sam said. Margaret sat back with a beaming smile on her face. She loved her husband and son more than anything in this world.

"I'm going upstairs to take out my outfit for tonight," Margaret said as she kissed them both."

West Philadelphia... Marriott Hotel parking lot...

Quincy pulled up, parked his tinted black Ford Mustang, and patiently waited. A few moments later, a grey Dodge Charger pulled up and parked beside his car. Inside were two off-duty police officers who had both been on Face payroll for years. Quincy rolled down the window and passed a small envelope to the passenger. "Vince, Nate, that's for the month, and I put a little something extra in there for the tips about the FBI raids," Quincy said.

"No problem. Just call when you need us," Vince said before rolling up the window and driving away.

Quincy pulled off behind them but made a left turn in the opposite direction. He was headed to meet up with a few other allies. It was his job to keep the streets in order, and he did it with cash and an iron fist.

CHAPTER 19

South Philadelphia

Inside his lavish condominium, Black Gotti and his right-hand man, Marvin, were sitting on the sofa discussing the business on the streets. "Our workers on the streets are complaining that there's no work out there," Marvin said as he puffed on a blunt.

"Well, one thing we don't do is ever question Face. His words are law, so let them complain," Gotti replied.

"If he tells us to stop moving product, then we stop!" he added. Marvin nodded his head in agreement and continued to smoke on his blunt. They were two drug bosses who knew the rules of the game and understood the assignment. No one disobeyed Face.

Chestnut Hill...

After hanging up the phone with his genius computer hacker, Marvin, Face took a long hot shower, dried himself off, and then lay across the large king-sized bed. The warm air from the fireplace felt good on his skin. Face lay there in deep thought. Strategically putting a master plan together inside his head. He was the ultimate chess player, not on the board, but in life, where every move was critical.

His thoughts quickly shifted to his late partner, Reese. There wasn't a day that went by that he didn't think of him. Life without him was hard, but as the years came and went, the pain eased. After speaking to his wife and children, Face turned on his reading light and reached and grabbed one of his favorite books. The 21 Lessons of Life by Jimmy DaSaint was his choice.

The beautiful island of Antigua was like heaven on Earth. Surrounded by the clearest, bluest water in the Caribbean. Tasha and her children were staying at the luxury beach mansion that Face had given Tasha for her birthday. The home had eight rooms, a full staff of cooks and waiters, and a six-car garage. Plus, there was a large pool and basketball court out back.

There were also two security guards that constantly roamed the property. Unbeknownst to Tasha, she was being secretly watched. In the shadows of the beautiful island was a person on an evil mission. He was consumed with hate and was ordered to kill Face's entire family. His name was Oliver Jenson. A highly skilled professional who worked for Sergio Miller. With over 50 confirmed kills, Oliver was itching to add a few more names to the list.

CHAPTER 20

Eastern Pennsylvania

Lodge #5 Pennsylvania Chapter... 10:15 pm...

Inside the large two-hundred-year-old historic building, over a hundred men and women were dressed for the night's special occasion. The large ballroom was filled with professionals from all over the East Coast. There were a few federal and district Judges, Governors, Mayors, Lawyers, Entertainers, Athletes, and a handful of high-level politicians. The room was filled with wealth and power. A lot of young faces with unlimited old money.

Seated at the front row, in front of the stage was Sam and his wife Margaret Livingston. They had been members at the lodge #5 for over forty years. Beside them were other top members of the #5 chapter. Across the stage was a large white banner that read, KNIGHTS OF LIBERTY. Lodge #5 was the Pennsylvania chapter of the Ku Klux Klan. They no longer wore long white sheets and white masks over their faces. Now, they wore expensive tailor-made suits and long dresses from the best fashion designers in the world. Many of the members had been born into this life.

The Knights of Liberty was one of the largest and most prominent chapters in the entire U.S. They secretly supported all the neo-Nazi groups in the United States, privately funding their evil agendas. They despised homophobic, Islamophobic, blacks, Asians, and the LGBT communities. On a wall was a large swastika flag and an American flag that was half burned.

Suddenly, two large doors opened, and Mark and a group of his closest friends walked in. Leo Renolds, Sergio Miller, Ken Nelson, his private investigator, and his lawyer Carter Samuels. They were all escorted and seated in the front row next to other high-ranking members of this secret society of wealth and hate.

As the lodge #5 President stood at the podium speaking, all eyes and ears were focused on every word that came out of his mouth. He was a tall, white, blue-eyed man in his late 60's. Each word that came out of his mouth penetrated every soul inside the room. His name was Edward Preston. Not only was he the highest-ranking member of the chapter and President for the last twenty years, but Edward Preston was also a U.S. Senator. A Republican who headed the Homeland Security and Governmental Affairs Committee. And a very close friend of the President of the United States.

CHAPTER 21

Bethesda Maryland

A few days later...

The sky was a calm blue with just a light wind blowing through the trees. Inside the Bethesda Meeting House Cemetery, there were hundreds of mourning family and friends. Most of them were still shocked by the tragic murder of the beloved Taylor Mitchell. Taylor was a well-known investment banker and property owner. All throughout the East Coast, his company represented some of the wealthiest people. He was known as "The man that made the rich richer."

With personal assets over 1.5 billion, Taylor was also one of the top 100 wealthiest Americans. Unbeknownst to Taylor, there was an enemy who disguised himself as a friend and wanted all that Taylor had earned. Mark Livingston walked through the crowd like a smooth pimp without a single care in the world. Right beside him was Sergio Miller, each man dressed in tailor-made black suits. Mark approached a beautiful white woman. She stood around 5 foot 10 inches, with long black hair. Her name was Amy Mitchell, the widow of Taylor. Mark gave Amy a long hug and whispered into her ear, "I'm truly sorry about your loss, and I give you my word: I won't stop until I find out who is responsible."

Amy looked Mark deep into his piercing blue eyes and said, "Thank you so much, Mark. And later, let's discuss those beach properties in Florida." Mark smiled and shook his head. They both knew that lots of eyes were watching and paying attention. After another hug, Mark and Sergio walked away. Before leaving the cemetery, they hugged and shook hands with other wealthy and prominent people. The fact was, not a single soul there suspected or had a clue that the man behind Taylor's murder and the man who put the bullet in his head was right there. They were evil at its finest, sons of Satan himself. Ruled by money, power, and greed. Men who played the game of life or death.

CHAPTER 22

Island of Antigua

12:18 A.M...

Only the bright, shining stars could be seen in the dark sky. The entire island seemed calm and tranquil. Most islanders worked hard and kept to themselves. Still, the beauty of Antigua had many secrets. While the shadows of evil men roamed around in complete silence. Oliver Jenson made sure he did his homework. He had paid off the right people that got him all the info he needed to finish his job. Dressed in all black, Oliver had secretly entered onto the beach property. With a loaded 9 mm silencer and mask on, he maneuvered throughout the grounds.

Soon, he came across the two security guards who were standing outside, taking a smoke break. Without hesitation, Oliver lifted and aimed his weapon. After pulling the trigger twice, he watched as both men slumped to the ground. An instant headshot killed them both. Oliver approached the men and shot them both once more in the face. Then he continued on towards the house. He had orders to eliminate Face's entire family.

Orders that he was excited to carry out. After climbing through a small back window, Oliver tip-toed inside the large, opulent mansion. Unbeknownst to Oliver, there were hidden security cameras placed all over the house, and every move of

Oliver was recorded. With his hand gripped on the gun, he slowly tip-toed up the stairs.

Downtown Philadelphia...

Face walked into his luxurious condominium and sat down on the soft sofa. After a long, busy day, his mind was consumed by lots of thoughts. Parked right outside his condo were two of his top bodyguards. Face knew that a man's safety added years to his life. After taking a long hot shower, he got in bed and closed his eyes. Even with his eyes closed, his thoughts would not go away. He didn't like this feeling, and Face knew that he had to do something about it. Sooner than later.

CHAPTER 23

The Ritz-Carlton Hotel

Washington DC....

The loud moans of a beautiful female swept all throughout the room. The hard, intense penetration she was receiving was much needed. Orgasm after orgasm ran all throughout her tall, slim body. Inside the dimly lit room, Mark had Amy Mitchell bent over the king-size bed. Every thrust of his dick made her scream with pure ecstasy. With his hand gripped around her neck Mark fucked her asshole. "Bitch, cum all over this dick!" he told her.

"Yes, Daddy! Yes," she yelled out. For over two years, Mark had been fucking the former Miss U.S.A runner-up and now the widow of Taylor Mitchell. She was one of many beautiful, successful women who shared his bed. Mark looked into Amy's green eyes and said, "Did you enjoy that?"

"Yes, I always do. No one has ever satisfied both of my holes like you," she said with a smile. Mark kissed her on the tip of her nose and said, "That husband of yours never fucked you like I do."

"Never!"

"When can we take care of that business? I'm ready to get this started."

"As soon as possible, babe. I'll have my lawyers reach out to Carter early in the morning. So after all the paperwork is signed, you should be the new owner of all beach properties in Florida," Amy replied with a smile.

Mark smiled and stood up. He then pulled Amy up, and they kissed passionately. In one motion, he turned Amy around and threw her down on her stomach. After spreading her long legs, Mark slid his hard dick back into her wet ass. In the calm of the night, her moans continued to fill up the room.

CHAPTER 24

Face reached over and answered one of his three burner phones.

"Hello."

"Baby, there's someone inside the house," Tasha whispered into the phone. Face quickly sat up with a terrified look on his face.

"Are you sure?"

"Yes, babe, I see him coming up the stairs on the video monitor in the bedroom," Tasha replied nervously.

"Where are the children?" he asked as he stood up from the bed and started putting on his clothes. He was filled with fear but he knew that he needed to stay calm for his wife.

"Did you press the security button?"

"I did; no one is answering," Tasha replied in a low whisper. As she talked to Face on the phone, she could see the shadowy figure walking slowly down the hallway toward the bedroom door. Fear swept all throughout her body. Face remained quiet on the phone. He didn't want the intruder to know that they had been talking on the phone. Suddenly, the bedroom door cracked open. Inside the dark bedroom, Tasha could see a large, bulky shadow figure enter the room. Without hesitation, she aimed and pulled the trigger. Bow!!! The bullet from the .40 hit the head of the intruder, and his large body slumped hard to the floor. As he lay there twitching in pain, it was obvious that he was still alive. Tasha stood over his body and shot him once more in the head. Leaving brain matter all over the expensive carpet. She quickly and nervously picked up the phone, "I did it, babe! I shot him twice in the head!"

"Good job, babe. Now I want you to call the local authorities, then get the kids and get out of that house. I'm going to make a few calls to make sure y'all are all okay. I'll be there in a few hours after I call Quincy to get the Jet ready. I love you, babe, you did great," Face said before he ended the call. Tasha walked around the dead corpse and ran down the hallway to her children's room. As she got them out of their beds, they all rushed out of the house.

CHAPTER 25

7:15 A.M...

The V.C. Bird International Airport was located on the island of Antigua and Barbuda. When the white Gulfstream jet landed on the runway, Face and Quincy quickly got off and rushed into a waiting all-black, tinted Mercedes Maybach GLS-SUV. They headed to the local police station, where Tasha and his children were all waiting. Once there, Face rushed into the small building. Seeing his wife and scared children standing, he couldn't help but shed a tear.

"Are y'all okay?"

"We're fine, babe. We're all good," Tasha said as they all stood there in a group hug.

"The captain would like to talk to you, a short black officer said to Face."

"I'll be right there," Face said.

When the officer walked away, Face asked Tasha, "What did you tell them?"

"Nothing besides an intruder came into the house, and I shot him. They watched the video and saw that the man shot and killed both security guards and climbed through a back window to enter the house," Tasha said.

Face nodded his head, and then he and Quincy followed a waiting officer into the Captain's office. Quincy shut the door behind them as Face and the Captain shook hands and sat down. "What can you tell me, Captain? Who was the man that entered the home with my wife and children?"

"Mr. Smith, we checked the man's passport, and his name is Oliver Jenson. He arrived on the island a few days ago. We did recover a cell phone on him, but none of the numbers could be traced to anyone. It's like the man is a ghost. We searched all our international records, and we couldn't find anything on Oliver Jenson," the huge, black Captain said.

"What about the case?"

"Open and shut. There will be no investigation. Oliver entered the home after killing two security guards. Then he was shot twice by your wife," the Captain said.

"I want this entire case to disappear. I don't want any records of this incident to come out," Face said as he looked over and nodded to Quincy.

Quincy walked over to the Captain and passed him a small briefcase. The Captain opened the briefcase, and his eyes lit up from seeing all the stacks of blue-faced hundred-dollar dills staring at him. It was the most money he had ever seen. "No press! No media! Nothing! I want this entire case to go away," Face said to the Captain.

"It's done. The body is currently down at the morgue, but my people will take care of things. They know what to do," The Captain replied.

"Also, I'm going to need his passport and cell phone."

"It's all yours, Mr. Smith," he said, passing the bag to Face.

"Don't worry, none of the evidence has been tainted; my officers used latex gloves to secure the entire area."

"Good job," Face said. "Do you mind giving us a few minutes to make a call?" Face asked.

"Not at all," the Captain said as he and his officer walked out of the office.

Face took out his cell phone and dialed a line. "I need that favor you promised me," Face said.

"It's done; just give me the details, and it will all be taken care of, my good friend," the Spanish man said.

After Face had explained all the details, they ended the call.

"What do you think, Quincy?"

"I think it's a good move. They will all be safe down there," Quincy answered. Face stood up from his chair, and he and Quincy walked out of the office. He then pulled Tasha to the side and told her what he needed her to do. He reassured he that everything had been taken care of and that the kids would all be safe. Tasha never questioned her husband; what he said was law. She respected and loved Face more than anything in the world. If he wanted her and the children to go to the moon, she would book the first space shuttle headed to space. Her love for him was unwavering. Her love was so strong that if she had to die to save him, death would be pleasant.

CHAPTER 26

Chestnut Hill, Philadelphia

The next day...

"What do you mean he was murdered?" Mark asked in an angry voice. "How? When?"

"He was shot in the head down on the island. There wasn't too much info or details. That's all I was told when I called and talked to the authorities," Sergio said. "That was my best man!!" he added.

"Did he get to finish the job he was sent to do?" Mark asked.

"I'm not sure. All I know is Oliver was killed, and no one on that damn island is saying anything."

"Well, hopefully, nothing will come back to us. I don't need any fuck ups!" Mark said in a serious tone.

"We're fine. The cellphone is untraceable and the passport was a phony. All they have is the name Oliver Jenson, and only you and I know his real name and information," Sergio replied.

"Do you think I should send some of my people to the island to do a private investigation?"

"No. It will come back to us and maybe expose too much. Robert is a... I mean, Oliver is a casualty of war. He understood the dangers of his assignment. It was supposed to be a covert mission, but something went wrong, and we will never know what really happened."

"What about the body?" Mark asked.

"We'll leave it and let the islanders decide on what to do with it," Sergio replied in a sad voice.

"I'm sorry about your friend, Sergio. He was a good, loyal soldier and also a new member of the Knights of Liberty, so this hurts me deeply. Hopefully, he got to Face's wife and kids before he was murdered. My priorities haven't changed; I want Norman "Face" Smith Jr. destroyed and his entire bloodline eliminated. I won't stop until I'm spitting on his grave, and I own everything he has," Mark said in a serious tone.

"How was your night? You didn't answer any of my calls?" Sergio asked as he changed the sensitive conversation.

"It's always good when you fucking a former Miss U.S.A contestant in the ass," Mark smiled. "Carter took care of all the necessary paperwork early today. Now, all the Florida beach properties belong to me. In five years, I'll be the biggest landowner in the entire state. I'm already good friends with the Governor. He'll be on board," Mark said as he reached for the TV remote and turned on CNN.

CHAPTER 27

Carlos Mendosa was one of the wealthiest drug lords on the planet. He was the leader of the Mendosa Cartel, which was associated with the powerful Sinaloa Cartel in Mexico. The Mendosa Cartel was the world's largest cocaine producer, and their top US distributor was Face. Even though he was no longer on the front lines of the drug trade, Face was the man behind so many big-time drug bosses across America.

Over the past five years, Carlos and Face had built a strong relationship. As Face, his family, and Quincy stood at the airport bunker, they waited for Carlos' private jet to land smoothly on the runway. Face and his family boarded the jet, and then he and Carlos stepped to the back of the plane to talk. "Thank you so much for this, Carlos."

"It's not a problem, my good friend. I promise to take good care of your family," he said in his Spanish accent.

"I'm sure they will be fine down in Columbia. I promise this current matter will be resolved very soon," Face said in a serious voice.

"Take your time, my good friend. Just know that I'll treat your family like I treat my own. With lots of love."

After kissing his wife and kids, Face and Qunicy exited the jet and watched as it flew off the runway, heading to Santa Marta, Columbia. "We have to hurry and get back to Philly so Marvin can find out who is this Oliver Jenson guy. I'll have my forensic analyst check for any prints on the passport and cell phone," Face said.

After finalizing all the paperwork for the beachfront properties down in Florida, Carter Samuels couldn't help but smile. He couldn't believe it, as once again, Mark had somehow swindled away another lucrative property. There was not enough money, power, or land that would satisfy Mark's greed. Carter had known every secret in Mark's life. All the good and ugly. Carter was the only person to whom Mark gave authorization to sign off on important documents. Because of their trusted friendship, Mark made carter a wealthy man.

After leaving the downtown office, Carter got into the waiting tinted black Lincoln SUV. Inside was a beautiful, petite Asian woman. Carter sat back and watched as the woman slowly undressed. He began to get excited and turned on. When the woman got undressed, Carter sat back with a huge smile on his pale white face. The Asian woman was a transgender with breasts and a dick. In the backseat of the SUV, Carter placed the man's dick in his mouth.

All throughout the wealthy community of the rich and famous, Carter was known as an undercover homosexual. He had black, Spanish, and Asian male lovers all up and down the East Coast. After their half-hour sex session, Carter had his driver drop the Asian transgender back off at home. As the SUV pulled up and parked in front of Carter's large 5-bedroom home, Carter fixed his clothes and got out. As soon as he walked inside the house his wife of over 30 years welcomed him with a kiss and a long hug.

Leo Renolds sat at his desk going over some very important paperwork that he had just received from the President. Being the US Attorney General had its perks, but the work was very tedious. The US Attorney General had to oversee all legal matters and generally gave advice and opinions to the President and other department heads of the executive departments of Government. With 92 US Attorneys under his leadership, Leo was a man of great power and influence. Feeling the vibration of his personal cellphone, Leo answered the call. "Talk to me, Mark. What's going on?"

"Our shadow man was eliminated down in the Caribbean," Mark replied.

"How? He had one job to do," Leo responded in a low whisper.

"We haven't gotten all the details, but the local authorities said that he had been shot."

"By who?"

"At the moment, none of that information is available. It's been hard getting anything out of those people," Mark said. "Is there anything you can do?" he added.

"I can make a few calls, but lately, it's been hard dealing with islands down the Caribbean. They can basically do as they want and please. The local governments are being paid off by the Colombians, Cubans, Mexicans, and some corrupt American criminals. So, I don't think it would be a wise move to have my guys go down there asking any questions. Plus, we don't need the FBI or the CIA in our affairs," Leo told him.

"I understand, I'm just pissed."

"As long as his real identity isn't known and nothing traces back to you, you're fine, my friend. Right now, I have to get ready for a Supreme Court briefing. I'll see you at the next lodge meeting, and we'll talk more in person," Leo said before ending the call. Leo and Mark had been friends for years. He had no problem abusing his power for Mark. Secretly, Mark had set Leo up with a private offshore account, where he was paid a substantial amount of money every month. So, the truth was that Leo was another powerful official on Mark's payroll.

CHAPTER 28

Fairmount Park, Philadelphia

2:23 PM...

Frank "Underworld" Simms, Simon "Black Gotti" Carter and Darius "King" Smith were all standing around discussing the business of the streets. They were all losing millions by the day after Face had called a shutdown of all drugs being moved in and out of Philly. As the three drug kingpins stood talking around, a brand-new Silver Porsche Cayenne pulled up and parked beside Frank's all-black Tesla Model X.

The door opened, and out walked a tall, handsome man dressed in a black Nike sweatsuit. His name was Carlos "Sosa" Williams Jr. Like all the men before him, he was a drug kingpin with a lot of power on the North Philly streets. Everyone greeted Sosa with handshakes. He was well-respected by all his peers.

"Any word yet from the big man?" Sosa asked.

"Not yet, but I'm expecting a call from him later today. He had to take an emergency trip out of the country," King said.

"The Feds have been raiding all my spots. I'm losing close to a million dollars a week with this shutdown. Who can have this much power over Face? His money and power are limitless," Sosa said in a confused voice.

"Someone with more money and power!" Gotti answered.

"Face will fix it just like he has done so many other times. I'm one hundred percent positive that Face is working on something major. We all know him and his capabilities. Face will not let anyone control him. He's always been the main piece of the chessboard," King replied. Sosa nodded his head in agreement.

"Well, to be honest, right now, my record label is doing great with all the success of my pop star diva Ashley Jay. I'm good for now. The Feds' surprise audit came up clear and good," Frank said with a smile.

"The truth is that we all have money put up for a rainy day. Right now, it might be storming a little, but not one of us is starving for any money. We are all loyal men of honor, and if we have to wait a year until things are back in order, then so be it," Sosa said.

"Right, money don't control us; we control the money", Gotti responded.

After their conversation had ended, each man got back into his luxury car and drove off in different directions.

King dialed a number on his cell phone, and a familiar voice answered. "How did everything go?" Face asked.

"All is well. The men are all loyal and understand that what's being done is mandatory. Your friend Sosa showed up as well," King told him.

"He's a good man. I was very close to his late father. He's very intelligent as well," Face said.

"Yeah, he's cool. I met him at your last birthday party you had on the yacht in Miami," King said, as he pulled up and parked in front of his condo.

"So why did you have to leave the country?"

"I had some personal business to take care of down in the Caribbeans."

"Is everything fine?" King asked.

"Yes, all is well," Face said, not trying to say too much. "Just continue to stay on point and keep your eyes and ears to the streets. We don't need no slip-ups. Remember, the Feds are always watching," Face told King before he ended the call.

"You good?" Quincy asked Face as he saw the concerned look on his face.

"I'm fine, Q. Bruce Lee once said, Emotions can be the enemy. If you give in to your emotions, you lose yourself. You must be at one with your emotions because the body always follows the mind."

Quincy shook his head in agreement. He was always impressed with Face's knowledge and understanding of people and the world. "Did Marvin find out anything yet from the passport name and cellphone?"

"He's still at his office working on everything. He said that a friend of his who works at an independent forensic laboratory in Jersey is analyzing the cell phone, and we should find out something by the end of the day," Quincy answered.

"Good, because we need to find out who Oliver Jenson is and who did he work for," Face said. "Do you think he's connected to Mark?"

"Who knows? He could've been there to rob the house, but I'm sure Marvin will find out something," Face said as he sat there thinking about his family.

"One thing for sure and two things for certain is whoever was behind the attack on my family will pay with their lives. Right now, they're all safe down in Colombia. Carlos will protect them as his own, and nothing goes down in Colombia without him knowing." Quincy's cell phone started ringing, and he answered, "Wassup?"

"I got something. Y'all need to come by my office ASAP," Marvin said excitedly.

"We on our way," Quincy said before ending the call. "Marvin got a hit, let's go." Face and Quincy rushed out the door, headed to Marvin's house.

CHAPTER 29

Chinatown

After returning back to Philadelphia from Hong Kong, Lee Chao was very upset and disturbed by the news he was hearing from his crew of Asian criminals. Lee was the biggest Asian drug lord on the East Coast. He had an illegal drug business in New York, Boston, Baltimore, and Philly. Mostly pushing illegal pills, heroin, and cocaine through all his underground drug channels and connections. "So why I'm not making any money? I have my bosses back in China that want and need answers," Lee said.

"The entire city has been ordered to shut down all the drug activity," Chen said, who was one of Lee's top men. "And who gave such an order?" Lee asked with a confused look on his face. "Face gave the shutdown order," Chen replied. Lee stood there in silence for a moment. He knew exactly who Face was. Even though he had gotten his drugs from sources out of China and Mexico, he was well aware of Face's power and reach. Lee stood there contemplating his next move. He was in a bad position to be in, but there were bigger black players in his homeland who depended on the money he sent them. "So what are we going to do?" Chen asked.

"The streets are dry right now. If we put some work out there, we will quadruple our money. Every hustler in the city would have to buy from us." Lee told him.

"But what about Face? He runs Philly. Plus, all the top Kingpins in the city and tri-state work with him. It would start a war," Chen said.

"A war we don't need," another Asian man added. Lee approached both men and said, "Do you think I give a damn about some nigger? I don't care who he is; to me, he's just another nigger in my way. I'm not letting Face or none of his nigger friends stop me from getting my money. I'm a soldier of the Triads. We are the most powerful gang all throughout Asia and the Far East. We bow down to no one. Not the white man and definitely not a nigger!" Lee yelled out. At the same time, all the men inside the room raised their right arms and shouted, "Triads! Triads! Triads! Triads!" Lee had made up his mind and was willing to deal with any consequences that came with his decision to move drugs throughout Philly.

CHAPTER 30

Northeast Philadelphia

Marvin was sitting at his desk staring into his computer monitor when Face and Quincy walked into his computer lab. "What's going on, Marvin?" Face asked as he sat down. "I found something on the guy Oliver Jenson. After some thorough research on the internet and the black web, I discovered that Oliver Jenson is an alias for a man named Robert Hill," Marvin said with excitement.

"Who is he, and who does he work for?" Face asked.

"I found out that Robert Hill is a former Navy seal. A few years ago, he was working for a private security firm in New York," Marvin said as he typed on the keyboard and showed Face and Quincy a digital folder of Robert's pictures. "There's a lot more!" Marvin said; as he clicked on the mouse, the screen on the monitor changed. "Robert is a member of a secret society called the Knights of Liberty. They are a group of wealthy men and women that secretly promote Neo-Nazis and so much more. They have a main chapter right outside of Ardmore, Pennsylvania."

"So why does this matter to us?" Face asked. Marvin clicked on the mouse, and a group photo of all white men appeared.

"As you can see in the photo, Robert is standing next to Mark Livingston, Leo Renolds, Carter Samuels, Sam Livingston, Sergio Miller, and US Senator Edward Preston. They are all members of the Knights of Liberty."

"So Robert works with Sergio. If it's true, then he also works for Mark," Face said. "Good job, Marvin."

"Also, my friend down at the forensic lab said that Robert Hill's fingerprints were on the passport and cellphone. Plus, one of the numbers on the cellphone was able to be traced to a home in Villanova, PA."

"Whose home is it?" Quincy asked. "The home is just one of the properties that belongs to Mark Livingston. So, my conclusion is that Mark and Sergio are both behind the murder attempt of your wife and children. They have the resources and funds to find out mostly everything about you. I'm sure they didn't have a problem finding your family down in the Caribbean," Marvin said.

Face nodded his head in silence, then he spoke, "So this man tried to murder my entire family!! Now the gloves are off! Everyone must die!"

"Yes, especially all them Ku Klux Klan motherfuckers", Quincy added.

CHAPTER 31

Santa Marta, Colombia

The eight-bedroom estate sat in the middle of twenty acres of pristine land. The exquisite home was lavish beyond all measure. It had an Olympic-sized pool, a basketball court, a tennis court, a spa, a bowling alley, and so many more amenities. The home also had a helicopter landing pad and a ten-car garage adjacent to it. Down inside the basement was a high-tech control center, with 20 computer monitors being viewed 24 hours a day by a staff of computer technicians.

Situated all around the property was a well-trained security team equipped with the latest gear and guns that would eliminate any intruders. As the kids were inside eating lunch, Tasha sat on an outside patio by the pool. All she could think about was her husband. He was her world, and the thought of being without Face created a fear like nothing she had ever felt or known.

Carlos saw Tasha sitting by the pool and approached her. When he sat down beside Tasha he could see that she had been crying. Worry was written all over her beautiful brown face. "Stop worrying. Face is a smart, good man; trust me, he'll be just fine," Carlos said in his Spanish accent.

"I know, Carlos, but since I've known him, it's never been this bad. No one has ever come for his family. Me and my children could've been killed inside that house," Tasha said as the tears rolled down her eyes.

"I understand; my late wife and daughter were kidnapped and murdered some years ago. The pain has never left my soul," Carlos told her. "But I understand this life we live in. We all know the consequences, and our enemies will stop at nothing to bring us down. Even if they must use our family to get to us."

Tasha sat there listening as Carlos continued to talk. She could tell that he was a very wise and intelligent man. His words gave her some relief and comfort. When the conversation ended, Tasha felt and knew that she and the kids would be safe, and she had no more reason to worry.

CHAPTER 32

Northeast Philly

Marvin was filled with excitement. He had just hacked into the U.S. Navy's main database. In less than 60 seconds, he was able to gather and collect some vital, disclosed military information. He picked up his burned cell phone and quickly called Face, who answered on the first ring. "Wassup, Marvin?"

"I found some very important information that you should know about," he said excitedly.

"Talk to me."

"Well, after an hour of figuring out some codes, passwords, and other info, I managed to break into the Navy's main database."

"What did you find?" Face asked.

"I found out that Robert Hill was a part of an elite Navy Seal team. The team had carried out covert missions in Afghanistan, Russia, North Korea, and Pakistan."

"Okay, that's good stuff," Face said.

"That's not all," Marvin replied.

"There's more?"

"Lot's more," Marvin answered. "Do you know who Robert Hill's chief commander was?"

"No, but I'm sure you're going to tell me," Face said.

"His chief commander was U.S. Senator Edward Preston! It's like they're all connected!" Marvin told Face.

"So Robert Hill was in an elite team of Navy seals that was overseen by Senator Edward Preston?"

"Yes. Edward Preston had served 30 years in the military before he got into politics. This is wild. The Knights of Liberty is like the next generation of the Illuminati. Ran by some of the most powerful, influential people in America."

Face sat back, listening to every word from Marvin's mouth. At the same time, his mind was racing with thoughts. He had to figure things out soon, or else the empire he built from his blood, sweat, and tears would crumble before him.

"So they are all connected, huh?" he asked.

"Yes, every single one of them," Marvin said.

"Well, just like a long line of dominoes. When one gets knocked down, the entire line begins to fall," Face said in a serious tone.

CHAPTER 33

Chinatown

Lee Chao watched as his men loaded barrels of pills, guns, and drugs into secret hidden departments inside ten white vans. They were getting ready to flood the streets of Philly and the entire tri-state. Lee knew that the streets were dry, and he was in a position to take over. Hidden inside the vans were over a million opioid pills. One hundred kilos of cocaine and forty kilos of heroin, with a street value of thirty million. Lee knew that his bosses back in China would be very pleased, and he would be promoted to an even higher position in the Triad criminal organization.

Washington, D.C...

The U.S. Capitol building housed the meeting chambers of the Senate and the House of Representatives for over two centuries. Senator Edwards Preston walked the halls as if he owned the place. He was respected by all his peers. He kept a stern look on his face and carried himself as a very poised and serious individual. Many of the other Senators and House Representatives knew about and understood the power he possessed. His hand controlled the strings of many of the most powerful men and women in Washington, D.C.

The former Navy commander wasn't just respected, but he was also feared. Knowing that Edward Preston was the leader of the secret society Knights of Liberty, there was not one single person in the Capital that he couldn't influence or erase. Inside his office, Senator Edwards was surrounded by three other Senators. Each man was from the Republican Party and also members of the Knights of Liberty.

"Why do we have to continue to pass legislation that constantly helps the niggers, spics, and white trash!" he yelled. "How much after-school funding and resources do those people need?

"The Democrats believe it helps move the country forward," one of the men said.

"Forward? They are tearing this once great country apart! We gave them COVID relief funds, and they spent it all on jewelry, cars, and drugs. We send billions to all the major cities, and the local city officials spend it on crap or steal it. It's all a damn scam, and I'm tired of it," Edward said in a frustrated voice. "We need an all-white America. With only the rich and wealthy a part of it," he added.

Downtown Philadelphia...

After the security guard locked up everything at the office, he escorted Janet out the front door. She walked down the street to the nearby Starbucks, sat, and ordered a Frappuccino. As she sat there scrolling through her cell phone, a tall, muscular, handsome black man approached her. "Excuse me, queen, but is anyone sitting in this seat?" he asked, showing his pearly white teeth.

"Nope, it's all yours," Janet smiled. Janet thought the man was very attractive, but she wasn't going to let him know that. She was sure that a man this fine, with light hazel eyes and a physic like a Greek God, could get any woman he wanted. "My name is Tyrone. You're a very beautiful woman," he said. "Well, I just started working downtown at the Credit Union on 12th Street," Tyrone said.

"Oh okay, I work just a few blocks away at the real estate building on 10th street," Janet replied. "Well, hopefully, we will run into each other a lot more," Tyrone said with a smile.

"Hopefully," Janet said, staring into his hazel eyes.

"How about we just exchange numbers? The next time we meet up, it will be planned," Tyrone said.

Janet thought about it for a few seconds and said, "Yeah, why not," then they exchanged numbers. After a brief conversation, they left Starbucks and headed in different directions. Janet was excited about the new handsome stranger. It had been over a year since she and her ex had broken up. When Tyrone got into his waiting Uber, he quickly dialed a number, and a male voice picked up on the first ring. "I'm in, boss," Tyrone said with excitement.

"Good job. Now you know what to do next. Your money will be deposited in your account in an hour," the man said before the call ended.

CHAPTER 34

140 S. Broad Street, Philadelphia

The Union League of Philadelphia is one of the city's most prestigious clubs for the wealthy. It boasted a rich history of influential members from the Philadelphia region. It was founded in the mid-1800s and has been a hub for top leaders in business, politics, and the arts. Dressed in a dark gray Armani suit, Mark was drinking with Sergio at the bar. "That was Lonnie on the phone, he's in," Sergio smiled.

"That's good stuff! Janet basically runs the whole operation over there. I'm sure she knows everything there is to know, so if Lonnie plays his part well, we'll be in right under Face's nose," Mark said.

"That's the plan. There are not too many women out here that can resist a man like Lonnie."

"You couldn't find a white man?" Mark said, sipping on his wine.

"From all the private investigating, our sources told me that she only liked her kind," Sergio replied.

"That's fine. Just after we get what we want out of him, you make sure to put a bullet in his head, too," Mark told Sergio.

"That was my plan all along," Sergio chuckled.

After a brief conversation, Sergio left Mark at the bar. He had an early morning meeting with a few of his men. While sitting in the lobby alone, two attractive blonde-haired women approached and sat beside Mark. Moments later, all three of them walked outside and got into a waiting BMW XM.

South Philly...

The white van was filled with twenty kilos of cocaine, ten kilos of heroin, and $200,000 worth of opioid pills hidden in secret compartments. When the driver pulled up at the traffic light at Broad & Snyder, he never knew that he had been followed by undercover FBI agents. Suddenly, a swarm of FBI cars and vans surrounded the vehicle. The Chinese driver quickly jumped out of the van, holding a loaded S-K semiautomatic. Knowing the consequences he would face if caught with all the drugs, he began shooting at the FBI agents' cars. When the agents returned fire, he was hit by a barrage of gunfire. Dying just a few feet away from the van. Once all the smoke and chaos cleared, there were four wounded agents and a dead Asian gangster. Just a few blocks away a second white van was pulled over by agents.

CHAPTER 35

The next day...

Senator Edward Preston had left Washington DC and made an early morning trip to Philadelphia to meet up with Mark at a secret location near Northern Liberties. "I'm opening up a new chapter for the Knights," the Senator said. "I'm going to need you to run the new chapter right here in Philly," he added.

"It would be an honor," Mark replied.

"Great. I'll also be starting a new chapter in Atlanta, Detroit, and Chicago as well," Edward said.

"What else will you need from me?" Mark asked.

"Like all the other chapters, I'm going to need your help funding and supplying our movement with the properties," Edward answered before sipping on a glass of scotch.

"That won't be a problem, Sir. I'll have Carter wire you all the funds in your private account that I had set up for you. Just give me a few hours."

Edward nodded his head with a smile; he already knew the answer before asking Mark the question. Mark was a devoted and dedicated member of the Knights of Liberty. The Knights had been a part of his family for years, and his parents were both high-ranking members. "Did you hear any new news on our man down in the Caribbean?"

"Nothing! The people in Antigua ain't saying anything," Mark replied.

"Well, it might be best to just leave it alone. Did you hear anything about the wife and kids?"

"Nothing, sir, it's like they just disappeared," Mark answered. Edward stood up and began to pace the floor.

"What's wrong?"

"There were lots of rumors in D.C. that Face is the man that was responsible for Senator C.W Watson's death a few years back. We had nothing that could bring him down," Edward said. "C.W Watson was a good friend of mine, and his death had been bothering me for years."

"Don't you worry, Face is going down, and I promise you that. Sooner than later, I'll own everything he has, and Norman "Face" Smith Jr. will be nothing but a memory," Mark said with confidence.

CHAPTER 36

Manayunk Philadelphia

Now living in a small one-bedroom apartment, Theodore Roberts was once one of the biggest real estate investors in Philadelphia. His company had a large real estate portfolio consisting of over 100 commercial and residential properties and other lucrative assets. At the time, Mark Livingston had offered Theodore an enormous sum of money to buy him out, but Theodore had turned his offer down three times.

Soon after, Theodore's life began to quickly crumble. First, an indictment by the Feds for a real estate fraud scheme. Then, a divorce from his wife after 25 years of marriage. Then, he ultimately had to file for bankruptcy. He lost it all: the money, cars, homes, his wife, and his children. Eventually, he had no choice but to sell his company to the one person he hated the most, Mark Livingston. A year later, Theodore found out that it was Mark and all his connections with major politicians and authorities who were behind his sudden downfall.

As Theodore sat there on the couch, beside him was a loaded .9 mm. For three days, he had been filled with suicidal thoughts. He was a man that was down on his past, and his future looked dim. Grief and sadness swept all through his short, pale, overweight body. All he did was sit around eating fast food while watching reruns of the TV show FRIENDS and FRASIER. All of his family and friends had abandoned him, and he felt there was nothing more to live for.

Theodore picked up the loaded gun and placed the barrel at his right temple. Today was the day to end it all, he said to himself. With his heart beating fast, his hand began to tremble. With each breath he took, he could feel the end coming closer. Suddenly, the sound of his ringing cell phone snapped him from out of his trance. The caller was unknown, but something told him to answer. "Hello, this is Theodore. Who is this?" he answered.

"How are you, Mr. Roberts? My name is Norman Smith, and I'm interested in hiring you for a job at my real estate firm downtown."

Theodore couldn't believe what he was hearing. At first, he thought it was a prank call or some type of joke. He knew exactly who Norman Smith Jr. was. The second largest real estate investor in Philadelphia. Only behind Mark Livingston. "Are you serious, Mr. Smith?"

"I'm a hundred percent positive, Mr. Roberts. I know all about your professional upbringing and background. You graduated from Drexel in '81 with a degree in Business Management. Started your company, The Roberts firm, right after college, featured in Time and Fortune magazine and so much more. I can keep going on, but just know that I did all my homework," Face said.

Theodore was very impressed but still in total shock. "When can I come in for an interview?"

"No need, you're hired. You can start in two days. You will have an office and your own secretary."

"What will be my job title?" he asked curiously.

"Head of Property Acquisition for the Philadelphia region, do you accept?"

"Yes! Yes! I'll be there early Thursday morning," he said excitedly.

"My secretary Janet will reach out to you in the next hour. Give her your address so she can send you some new suits and a driver that will pick you up from your home," Face said.

"I sure will, and thank you so much!" Theodore said as he put the gun down on the couch.

After the call ended, Theodore sat back, tears rolling down his face. He knew that it had to be a blessing from God. Face sat back looking over at Quincy with a big smile on his Face.

"It worked out well, I see," Quincy said.

"Sure did. The one thing I know is to always surround yourself with smart, intelligent people who can help you grow and teach us things. Plus, it don't hurt that I and Theodore have the same enemy, Mark Livingston," Face said with a serious look on his face.

"An enemy that has no idea his time is running out."

CHAPTER 37

For two days, Janet and her new handsome friend Tyrone Jones had been talking and meeting up after work. Each time, she could feel herself liking him more. Tyrone was not just handsome, but he was very intelligent as well. They found out that they had so much in common. Both were Geminis. Their favorite color was red, and neither of them had children. Plus, Tyrone was seven years older, and Janet always had a thing for older, mature men.

After dinner, they went back over to Janet's downtown Condominium near Arch Street. After another drink of Dom Perignon Champagne, they started kissing passionately. Janet was beyond turned on as her nipples perked through her silk white shirt. She grabbed Tyrone's hand and led him to her bedroom. After they both undressed, Janet lay there in total shock, as she couldn't help but stare at Tyrone's God-like body.

A few moments later, Janet was moaning out in pure ecstasy as Tyrone fucked her with aggressive passion and pure lust. His thick 9-inch dick had Janet calling God and begging for more. It was the best sex that she had ever had in all her life. So she lay there enjoying this new stranger take her mind, body, and soul to new heights.

"What do you mean there were a few major drug busts in South and North Philly?" Face said into the cell phone.

"I told everyone to shut things down for a while. Who the fuck disobeyed me?"

"It was Lee Chao from the Triads," Sosa said. "The FBI and DEA did a city-wide sweep, and some members of his crew got caught up in it," he added.

"What the fuck! Didn't you tell them that there was a shutdown city-wide?"

"I told his partner Chen. So I'm sure he knew," Sosa replied.

"This is fucked up, and it will only bring us more heat from the Feds! Heat that none of us need right now!" Face angrily said.

"What's wrong with that Chinese asshole?"

"He don't respect any of us, especially a black man," Sosa said. "Plus, he believes that he is invincible and unstoppable with all the manpower he has," Sosa added.

Face stood up from the sofa and paced back and forth in the living room. "Get the guys together; I have to make an example out of this nigga," Face said before ending the call.

CHAPTER 38

Philadelphia

Downtown, FBI office...

A plethora of drugs and guns were laid out on a large table. For the FBI, it had been a major drug bust. A group of local press members and national media were seated and standing around requesting interviews and taking pictures for different publications.

FBI agent Simon Kowoski stepped at the podium, holding a black folder. "As you all know, a few days ago, there were two major drug busts in the city. FBI agents were tipped off by a confidential informant, and an undercover task force arrested three individuals and confiscated over two million dollars' worth of illegal guns and drugs. Upon one of the arrests, Agents had to shoot one of the gunmen who was shooting at them. The man of Asian descent, whose name is Cho Ming, was killed at the scene. Records show that Cho Ming is a top member of the Triad criminal crime syndicate, based out of Hong Kong, China, with chapters up and down the East Coast. Informants also told us that the Triads are in business with all the top black criminals in the city. Knowing this information, we here at the FBI are determined to bring down every single criminal drug organization in Philadelphia. At the moment, we have a list that we will not disclose, but rest assured, we won't stop tracking all the criminals down until they are behind bars in a federal penitentiary."

Chestnut Hill, Philadelphia...

Inside his lavish home, Face, Frank Underworld, King, Sosa, Black Gotti, and Quincy all sat around watching the news on CNN. Face was livid, and everyone inside the room could feel his energy. He felt disrespected by Lee Chao and the Triads. The drug bust had put a target on everyone, and Face knew that he would be the biggest target. He was the boss of all bosses, and the Feds wouldn't be satisfied until they cut off the head of the snake. In a room full of silence, Face looked at everyone and said, "Only the dead have seen the end of war."

CHAPTER 39

The next day...

Ken Nelson had been secretly watching all of Face's employees coming and going from the building. He had taken notes on their times and dates. So far, he had gathered information on all the top employees' homes, banks and other outside activities. He was meticulous when it came to undercover investigations. His job was to gather all the information he could on Face's real estate firm. After typing down notes on his iPad, Ken started up his car and drove away. Still, once again Ken had no idea that a set of eyes knew exactly who he was and who he worked for and was watching Ken from the shadows.

New York City...

Outside the Plaza Hotel...

The city that never sleeps was wide awake with people. Large crowds of people flooded Manhattan on every street corner. On the corner of Fifth Avenue, Sergio sat inside a car screwing on the silencer to his .9 mm. He had come here to do a highly-paid job. His target was a Wall Street broker named James Wiggins. Six months earlier, Mr. Wiggins had mismanaged a large sum of money in a wealth portfolio he ran for Mark Livingston. For that mistake, his life was now in jeopardy.

Sergio watched as James and a female friend got out of a yellow cab. They had just seen a stage play down on Broadway. Dressed in a black leather jacket and a pair of matching leather gloves, Sergio stepped out of the car and began to slowly walk towards the happy couple. There were a few people outside, but their attention was focused elsewhere. Suddenly, Sergio pulled out his gun and started shooting at James and his female friend. Both of their bodies fell hard to the ground, each with multiple bullets in their unprotected heads. Death was silent and instant. Moments later, Sergio was back inside his car, headed back to Philadelphia. He quickly dialed Mark's private cell phone.

"Hello," Mark answered.

"It's done!" Sergio said.

"Good job. Right now, I'm at a black-tie event. I'll see you later tonight after the event is over. I have my eyes on something nice," he said before ending the call.

CHAPTER 40

Atlantic City, NJ

The Borgata Hotel Casino was elegant on all levels. Since opening in 2003, it's been the top-grossing casino in Atlantic City. Inside the huge, lavish ballroom, the black-tie event was filled with some of the wealthiest people in America. Athletes, entertainers, politicians, and celebrities were all gathered inside the ballroom, networking while enjoying the festivities.

When popstar sensation Ashley-Jay walked into the room, it seemed like the entire room froze. Her beauty was intoxication, and her aura demanded attention. At 5 feet 10 inches, with a gorgeous slim frame, long black hair touching the smalls of her back, and a face as flawless as a rare diamond. Ashley was drop-dead gorgeous with a voice straight from God himself.

Surrounded by two large bodyguards, Ashley sat down at her reserved table. Watching her every move was Mark Livingston. Dressed in a black Italian-made tuxedo, Mark wore his money well. With a bottle of Louis Roederer Cristal Champagne, Mark approached Ashley's table. 'He's kinda cute,' she thought to herself.

"Hey beautiful, do you mind having a drink with me?" He asked her, showing off his pearly whites.

Ashley looked him up and down and could tell that this man's entire aura said old money. From his Rolex Submarine watch to his Gucci shoes, he exuded wealth. "Sure, why not handsome," Ashley said as Mark sat down beside her.

The truth was that each of them had known who the other was. Ashley was a woman, and Mark had many thoughts about bedding. The lust in his blue eyes was evident. After they talked and had a drink together, they exchanged numbers and promised to stay in contact with each other. When Mark had left, Ashley quickly texted a number.

At the same time, Mark was texting Sergio:

THAT NICE THING I TOLD YOU I HAD MY EYES ON IS IN THE NET. I'LL BE FUCKING HER IN A WEEK.

The text read in all capital letters.

CHAPTER 41

Chinatown

10:45 PM...

The Chatayee Thai restaurant was one of the most popular spots to eat at in Chinatown. Tonight, there was a large crowd of partygoers there to celebrate Lee Chao's 35th birthday. Surrounded by all of the Triad gang members, Lee was having the time of his life. Two beautiful Asian women were wrapped around his arms. Half drunk, Lee began to get loud and boisterous. He ripped off his white t-shirt, showing the red dragon tattoo on his chest. This only made the crowd get louder and even rowdier.

Parked outside the restaurant was a long line of luxury cars, including Mercedes, BMWs, Lexus, Cadillacs, and an all-white Maserati. On the opposite side of the street were two parked Ambulances. The night was dark and calm, with just a few people out walking the streets. Lee had always been a man who played by his own rules. He knew that he was protected by one of the most powerful criminal organizations in the world.

After the party had ended, Lee and his two female acquaintances walked towards the exit door. Right behind them were all the members of his gang. Before they walked out, Lee's top street solider, Chen, went out first to check out their surroundings. Once he saw that the coast was clear, Chen led them out the door. Each of Lee's top men walked towards their parked cars. All headed back to a secret location where they did their illegal activities.

Suddenly, the back doors of the two Ambulances burst open, and four gunmen, dressed in all back, with masks covering their faces, began to unload their semi-automatic weapons. One at a time, each man fell dead to the ground. The only survivors were Lee and the females, but they quickly ran down the street screaming. A few feet away from Lee was his top man, Chen. Lying in a puddle of blood from a headshot. When Lee tried to run, he was quickly caught by one of the masked shooters. He dragged Lee over to one of the ambulances and threw him in the back. After closing the doors, both Ambulances sped off down the street.

With flashing red and blue lights, other cars moved out of the way to let it speed by. At the scene of the crime, there were twenty dead members of the Triads laid out in the streets. A crowd quickly gathered around all the dead bodies in total shock and disbelief. It was sure to be the deadliest mass murder in Philadelphia's history. The two Ambulances pulled up and parked in the back of a warehouse near Girard Avenue. The doors opened, and one of the men dragged Lee out by his jacket collar. He was scared and petrified, not knowing who it was that gun-downed his entire crew and kidnapped him.

They all walked through the warehouse into a back room. Standing there in an all-black Adidas sweatsuit was Face. Right beside him was his right-hand man, Quincy. Gripped in Face's hand was a loaded .357 magnum. The four men all took off their masks, each revealing who they were. It was Frank Underworld, Sosa, King, and Black Gotti. All the men were responsible for the gang hit and kidnapping. Sosa pushed Lee to his knees, a few feet away from Face's Adidas shell top sneakers. "Here you go, Face. Everything worked out just like you planned it. Like you said, Lee and his entire crew would be at his party," Sosa said. Face looked down at the short, skinny, timid man and could plainly see the fear in his eyes. While everyone stood around watching and waiting, Face said, "Don't you know to never share all of your business on social media? Blame today on Instagram."

"Please, Face! Please don't kill me! I'll pay you whatever you want! Just spare my life!"

"You broke a rule, and you purposely disrespected me. For that, you must pay the ultimate price, death," Face said as he aimed the gun at Lee's head. Face pulled the trigger, blowing pieces of Lee's brain on the cold ground. Then, Face and his crew walked away. Leaving Lee's body surrounded in a puddle of his own blood.

CHAPTER 42

Two days later...

After the brutal mass murder of the Triads, the whole city was talking. The local FBI office was in complete shambles and had agents out trying to get some answers. The Mayor and Philadelphia Police Chief were also searching for answers, as they placed even more officers out on the streets. Both the local and national news outlets ran with the story. "The Triads is a major crime syndicate. For someone to be this bold and take them out like this, they had to be involved with something so much bigger," FBI Agent Simon Kowoski said at a small press conference.

"Who could've done it?" a reporter asked.

"At the moment, we don't know that. But whoever it was was just as big as the Triads or even bigger. There are other big crime organizations in the city, but we haven't heard anything about a turf war between any of them. So right now, the FBI and local authorities, along with the Mayor and Police Chief, are joining forces to find some answers," Simon answered.

Downtown Philadelphia...

Theodore Robert was still in disbelief. Sitting at his desk inside his new office felt like a dream. Janet had made sure he was nicely set up and eased comfortably into his new position.

Just a few days earlier, he was contemplating suicide. Now, he was the head of acquisitions at one of the biggest real estate firms in Philly. After only a few days on the job, Theodore was mastering his job. He knew the real estate game like the back of his hand. He had even shown Face and Janet a few tricks he knew about. Face was very impressed with his new hire.

While Ken Nelson continued to take pictures and secretly investigate the people at the real estate office, he had no idea that Quincy secretly placed a GPS tracking device under his car. Back at his office, Marvin had been watching Ken's every move on his laptop. The shadow had no idea that he was being shadowed. As Ken sat back in his car, he noticed a familiar face come out of the building. He quickly took out his cell phone and snapped a picture. Then he sent the picture to Sergio. Moments later, a text from Sergio came to Ken's cellphone:

Is that Theodore Roberts?

Yes, he's working with Face right now. Ken texted back.

Thanks, Ken; keep up the great work. I'll let Mark know when he returns from his date. Sergio texted back.

CHAPTER 43

Center City

The Vetri Cucina restaurant was one of the best Italian restaurants in Philly. A place where only the wealthy hung out and ate. The food was great, and the staff were good at their job. Sitting at a private booth in the far back was Mark and Ashley. Mark had been asking her out on a date ever since they met, and Ashley finally gave in. A few tables away were two of Ashley's huge bodyguards. Making sure that no one tried to bum rush for an autograph. Ashley sat back, smiling while Mark flooded her with compliments. She was used to this kind of attention from wealthy men, athletes, and celebrities. With lust in his eyes, Mark was very persistent. He wanted to fuck Ashley badly, just so he could add another fine specimen to his long list of sex partners. "After dinner, why don't you come over to my Penthouse and get a drink and watch a movie?" he said.

"Mark, not tonight," she answered.

"Why not? I promise you'll have a wonderful time."

Ashley looked deep into Mark's blue eyes and said, "No, Mark, I promise you, baby, whenever I do decide to come over to your place, you will have a wonderful time. I'm good at a lot of things, not just singing," Ashley said with a serious look on her face.

Mark sat back, feeling himself being turned on. He wasn't used to women turning down any of his invitations. The more Ashley turned him down, the more Mark was turned on. After dinner ended, Mark walked Ashley to the door. She gave him a long warm hug and put her mouth to his ear, "Trust me, big boy, this pussy is going to be worth it." Then Mark stood there, turned on even more, watching as Ashley's bodyguards escorted her into the waiting, tinted black Mercedes Benz SUV. After taking a long, deep breath, Mark took out his cell phone. After one ring, a female voice answered, "Hey, baby."

"Hey Amy, I want to see you tonight. Meet me at my penthouse in an hour."

"Okay, I'll start getting myself together, call you back soon," she said before the call ended.

If I can't fuck the pop star tonight, then a former Miss USA runner-up will do, he thought.

CHAPTER 44

9:22 AM...

The next day...

"How is Carlos treating you and the children?" Face asked as he and Quincy sat in the back seat, driven around by one of the armed bodyguards.

"He and his family are all wonderful. They treat us with nothing but respect, and the staff are just amazing. It's beautiful down here, and I'm so glad you sent us here, baby. Is everything good back in Philly?"

"It will be," Face answered.

"Well, do whatever you need to do to fix whatever is broken. I trust you will, Face. I have one hundred percent faith in you, baby."

"I know you do, babe. Trust me, I'm on it," Face replied as the driver turned down Lancaster Avenue.

Sitting on the bed inside his lavish downtown Penthouse, Mark was talking on the phone with Sergio. Naked and still deep asleep was the former Miss U.S.A. runner-up, Amy Mitchell. "Is he sure it was Theodore Roberts Ken saw coming out of the building?"

"Yes, it's definitely him. He took pictures of Theodore coming and leaving," Sergio told him.

"So Theodore Roberts is working for Face now! I wanted that man buried!" Mark stood up and said. After putting on his black robe, he walked out of the bedroom and shut the door behind him. "When I destroy an enemy, I want him to suffer forever! Face is really pissing me off Sergio. He needs to go, and I need his company!" Mark yelled into the cellphone.

"Boss, it's taking a little longer than expected, but I'll get him, and you'll get his company. He's very well protected, and tracking him on a consistent basis has been difficult. It's like he's aware of what's going on, but trust Face is going to slip up, and when he does, my bullet will be the one that ends him," Sergio said in a serious tone. "What do you want me to do now?" he added.

"Just make sure that Ken keeps an eye on them all. What's up with Lonnie?"

"Oh, it's been good so far. He's been fucking the secretary all week long, and she's loving every moment of it," Sergio replied.

"Good; once he starts gathering some crucial info on the company, I want them both dead."

"It's already in my plans, boss," Sergio said before ending the call.

Chapter 45

Upper Darby, PA

Carter Samuels made sure that the Airbnb he rented was located in an undisclosed location right outside of Philly. He demanded his privacy so that he could perform all his freak sexual acts. Inside the bedroom, Carter was bent over the king-size bed being fucked by a 6ft 4inch black man. Despite his deep hatred for African American people, he couldn't fight his lust for a big black dick. As his moans and grunts filled the air, another black man walked into the room. He was a transgender, standing there with big firm breasts and a long hard dick. "It's my turn," he told the other guy.

"Oh, right now, I need a break," Carter said as he slumped down on the bed.

The transgender man walked up to Carter with a serious look on his face and said, "You paying us ten grand a piece to fuck you, so you're going to get fucked!" he said before sliding his dick into Carter's asshole.

Ardmore, PA...

Sam and his wife Margaret had just returned back home from another Knights of Liberty lodge meeting. They were long-time members, and so was their son Mark. Sam was actually the great-grandson of one of the founding fathers of the Virginia Ku Klux Klan. Hatred for blacks, Jews, Asians, and gays were breaded deep into his soul. He and his wife were now wealthy, retired philanthropists who supported and donated their money to organizations that supported the white race and their evil agendas.

"I'm so glad that that black asshole of a President is out of office. We need Trump back or at least someone like him," Sam said as they both sat down on the sofa.

"He's very lucky to be out of office; look what your friends did to Malcolm X and King. He would've been next for sure," Margaret replied.

Sam looked at his wife and said, "The key to bringing down their race is about taking away all of their hope. They might've built this country, but the white man mastered it all. Not just America, but the whole entire world!" Sam said, with a devilish look on his face.

"White power!" Margaret yelled out.

CHAPTER 46

Marvin sat at his desk, watching the large colored monitor. He was writing down all the locations where private investigator Ken Nelson had visited. Ken had no idea that Quincy had placed a GPS tracking device under his car. So far, Marvin had written down ten different places that Ken would frequent. Ken had no idea that he was being watched and that he was a critical piece of Face's chessboard.

Leo Renolds had been flooded with calls from the Chinese Embassy. Since the mass murder down in Philadelphia, there were some high official Chinese diplomats who wanted answers. So far, Leo or his staff didn't have any info to relay. Like so many others, Leo was dumbfounded. "I promise to get down to the bottom of this, Mr. Wong," Leo said into the phone. "I already have some of my best men in Philadelphia searching for answers as we speak," he added.

"Okay, Mr. Attorney General, I'm counting on you to get to the bottom of this matter. The Chinese government is very embarrassed by this tragedy," Mr. Wong said.

"Well, our sources in Philadelphia are saying that Lee Chao was a top member of the Chinese Triads crime organization. Is that true?"

"That's false! Lee Chao was an official diplomat for the Chinese government. He's had diplomatic immunity for over five years, so any accusations of being a part of a criminal organization is a lie," Wong replied.

"There will be a thorough investigation on this matter, and hopefully, the truth will be revealed. I'll call you with any new info," Leo said before ending the call.

Washington, DC...

Embassy of the People's Republic of China...

After ending the call with Leo, Mr. Wong looked over at two of his Chinese officials. "They are doing an investigation into the murders in Philadelphia. We don't need anything linking Lee back to the Triads. This would be very embarrassing, so I need y'all to make some calls to ensure that Lee is cleared and his record remains spotless. Our government doesn't need this incident to blow up in our face."

"We are on it, Sir!" One of the officials said before both men walked out the door. Mr. Wong took out his cell phone and made a call to someone back in China.

CHAPTER 47

The next day...

The tinted black Tahoe truck pulled up in front of Face's Chestnut Hill estate; waiting inside was the bodyguard driver and Quincy. Face walked out the front door and got inside his truck. He had an important meeting with all the heads of his company. Dressed in a black Armani suit, Face sat back, texting Theodore on his cell phone. As they drove through the city, Face looked out the tinted window. Memories of him and Reese running around hustling entered his mind. Driving through Germantown, North Philly, and Center City, Face could feel a Deja Vu. He had seen this day before, he thought to himself.

The FedEx truck had been parked across the street from the real estate building for two hours. Dressed in a FedEx uniform, Sergio Miller had been patiently waiting. Sitting on his lap was a Remington 300 sniper gun. He had gotten from Ken Nelson that Face would be in the office for a very important staff meeting. A few days earlier, Ken had managed to get some recorded conversations from a few high-level employees. So Sergio sat back, waiting for Face to show up.

A few moments later, the black Tahoe truck pulled up and parked in a reserved parking space. Standing outside the front of the building was another one of Face's bodyguards. He was armed with a Glock 19 9mm Luger. Quincy stepped out of the truck and carefully surveyed the scene. A few pedestrians were walking to work; other than that, it was a calm morning.

As soon as Face stepped out of the truck, the blast from a bullet shattered the front window, and his driver was instantly killed. When Quincy and the other bodyguard rushed over to cover Face, Quincy was shot in the shoulder and fell to the ground. The bodyguard pulled out his Glock and started to return fire. At the same time Face pulled out his 9mm and began shooting as well. They both watched as the FedEx truck sped off down the street.

Face quickly rushed over to Quincy and helped get him into the building for safety. They weren't sure if there were other shooters. A small crowd quickly gathered around the front of the building. Employees rushed outside in shock and disbelief. Face stood there with an angry look on his face. He had seen the driver's face before he sped off. This war had gone to another level, and now it was time to end it, Face thought to himself.

CHAPTER 48

Temple Hospital

A few hours later...

After being seen by the doctors and bandaged up, Quincy was released with just a minor flesh wound. A few more inches to the left, and the bullet would've hit him in the head. Quincy was livid, and if it wasn't for Face calming him down, he was ready to get his revenge on the man who had almost taken his life. Sitting inside a tinted BMW, Face and Quincy were talking. "We lost a good man today, and we both almost lost our lives!" Quincy said.

"I've already taken care of Mike's funeral expenses, and I made sure his family is set for life. But rest assured, Mark and his goon Sergio are going to regret the day that they tried to kill me at my office building!" Face said in an angry tone. "It's all over the damn news, and lord knows I don't want or need this kind of attention surrounding me right now," he added.

As they sat back talking, Face's private cellphone line started ringing. "Hello," Face answered. There was a long pause, and then a voice said, "So, Mr. Smith, are you ready to sell now? My offer is still available," Mark asked.

After a long sigh, Face said, "Do you know who you're playing with? Do you really think this is a game?" Sometimes your money and power can't save you, Mark! You barked up the wrong tree, and once again, I'll never sell my company to you!" *Click* The phone went dead.

Quincy looked over at Face and just shook his head. No one had ever antagonized Face before. Mark was lighting a powerful fuse that no one could put out. He had Face boiling with rage. "You ready?" Face asked.

"I have been ready," Quincy replied.

"I need you to tell Frank, King, Gotti, Sosa, and Doc that the time has come. I need them to all meet up at the condo in the morning."

"I'm on it!" Quincy said as the driver drove down Germantown Avenue.

"Is everything in place?" Face asked.

"Yes, Marvin gave me all the info we need. I have a list of names and addresses."

"Any word on the Chinese murders?" Face asked.

"Our friend down at the FBI office said that they are currently doing an investigation, but so far, they don't know who was responsible for the Triad gang's murder."

Face sat back, nodding his head. His mind was clouded with so many thoughts. As he sat back in anger, Face knew he had to stay calm and move smart.

CHAPTER 49

Early the next morning...

Inside Janet's downtown condo, she and Tyrone had just finished another intense round of sex. For the past week, they had been engaged in a nonstop sexual adventure. As Janet's naked body lay on the silk sheets, Tyrone slid his hand slowly up and down her spine. "Did you enjoy that babe?" Tyrone asked.

"Yes, I did. That thing you be doing with your tongue drives me crazy," Janet replied with a smile. As they continued to talk, Janet's cell phone started to ring. When she saw who it was calling her, she quickly answered, "Yes, sir, is everything okay?" she said on the phone. The voice on the other end instructed Janet on what to do. She then began to put back on her clothes and shoes. When she hung up, Tyrone asked, "Is everything okay, babe?"

"Yes, I just have to make a quick run; I'll be right back, so just relax until I return," she said. After Janet kissed Tyrone on the lips, she rushed out the door. As soon as she left, Tyrone began looking around her bedroom. He was searching for anything that was important so he could give it to Mark and Sergio. When Tyrone heard the front door open, he quickly got back in bed. Suddenly, the bedroom door opened and Janet, along with Face and Quincy, walked into the room. Tyrone instantly felt the rush of fear enter his body. Quincy aimed his loaded .40cal at Tyrone's head.

"You have some serious explaining to do, Lonnie. Your real name is Lonnie Wright, right?" Face asked.

"Please! I was paid to introduce myself to Janet and hopefully get some info out of her," Lonnie said in a scared voice.

"Is your name Lonnie Wright or not? And who do you work for?" Face asked silently.

"Yes, that's my name, and I work for Mark Livingston and Sergio Miller!" Janet stood back, speechless. She was angered beyond words. Just knowing that Lonnie had been playing her the whole time made her sick to her stomach.

"How did y'all find out?"

"I have my sources, Lonnie, but did you know that your bosses were also planning to kill you once you got whatever they needed? Do you know that this whole time, you were just a pawn? I check on all of my employees, so when you popped up in Janet's life, I had my people look you up, Lonnie. It took us some time, but we eventually found out everything about you," Face told him.

"Please! Please, I was just doing my job!" Lonnie yelled.

Janet looked into Lonnie's scared eyes and said, "Fuck you, nigga, I hope you get everything you deserve." Then, she walked out of the bedroom and left the apartment.

"I want you to call Sergio and tell him that you got some important info for him. I'm sure he would like that," Face said.

"Please don't make me do that!" Quincy placed the gun to Lonnie's forehead and said, "Do it or die!"

Lonnie weighed his options as he sat there shaking his head. "Okay, I'll call him now," Lonnie said, as he reached and grabbed his cell phone from off the nightstand. He quickly dialed Sergio's number and waited for him to pick up.

"Hello," Sergio answered.

"I got something for you. I think it will be beneficial to you and Mark. Can we meet up around six? We can meet up at the house," Lonnie asked.

"That's fine. I'll be there, and it better be worth it," Sergio said.

"Oh, it is, sir. You'll be proud of me," Lonnie replied.

"I'll see you soon," Sergio said before ending the call.

"Good job, now get dressed. You're going with us," Face said. After Lonnie had put back on his clothes and shoes, he was escorted by Quincy out of a back door.

A waiting black van was parked, and two of Face's armed men were inside. Quincy pushed Lonnie into the van, and then he and Face both got inside. Seconds later, the van pulled off down the street.

"Please! Please! I did what you asked," Lonnie begged.

Face looked at the scared, weak man and said, "You picked the wrong team to be on, Lonnie. The wrong team."

CHAPTER 50

Washington, D.C

Attorney General's Office...

Mr. Wong stood around 5 feet 4 inches tall, but he had the confidence and attitude of a man much bigger. Being a high-ranking diplomat at the Chinese Embassy gave him not only lots of power but immunity as well. The Chinese and the Russians were two of America's biggest nuclear threats, so it was in the U.S.'s best interest to be on good terms with members from both nations. Mr. Wong walked into Leo's office, leaving his two bodyguards standing outside the door. After shaking hands, both men sat down.

"Any new information?"

"Yes, we found Lee's body, and I already started the process of returning the body back to China. Also, after a thorough investigation by some of my top agents in Philadelphia, we believe it was a planned assassination by the Russian Mob," Leo said.

"The Russians!" Mr. Wong said shockingly.

"Yes, because there are some other crime organizations in and around Philadelphia, but only the Russians would have the men and capabilities to pull something like this off. Because, for one, none of the black drug organizations have the smarts or manpower to even attempt a hit like that. Trust me, they'd rather kill each other. Also, the attack outside the restaurant was done with Russian military machine guns. I believe the Russians and the Chinese were in a war over drugs and territory," Leo said.

Mr. Wong stood up, shaking his head in disbelief. "The Russians?"

"That's not all; after all the autopsy were done, we noticed that each man had a particular tattoo of a dragon on his back. After some research, we found out that it's a symbol of the Chinese Triads crime organization."

"And what does that have to do with anything?" Mr. Wong asked suspiciously.

"Lee Chao also had a dragon tattoo on his back," Leo replied. Leo could see the worried look on Mr. Wong's face.

"Don't you worry, Mr. Wong. I'll keep that info among us. I have no interest in embarrassing the Chinese government. We both know the truth that the Chinese were running a multimillion-dollar drug business here on U.S. soil, and the Triads were behind it all. And that Lee Chao is or was one of the top members. He was also a diplomat working at the Chinese Embassy," Leo said. Mr. Wong stood there speechless. He knew that the Attorney General had done his job well. He then reached out and shook Leo's hand. "So this information doesn't leave this office?"

"I give you my word, Mr. Wong."

Thank you, we'll talk soon," Mr. Wong said before leaving the office.

Leo sat back in his chair and took out a Cuban cigar. He knew a lot more than he told Mr. Wong. Leo knew all about the Chinese and Japanese crime syndicates that operated all throughout the U.S. He also knew that Mr. Wong was a spy for the Chinese government and Leo Chao was his nephew.

In less than a week, Theodore Roberts still couldn't believe how his life had changed overnight. He had gotten a new car and moved into a new home. He had even started talking to his ex-wife and children again. He was well-liked and respected by all the staff members. So far, his department had acquired twenty more commercial properties and two old, broken-down hotels that could be restored and sold. His knowledge of real estate investing was impeccable. Seeming to rub off on everyone around him. When Janet walked into the office, he noticed the sad look on her face. "Are you okay? I thought today was your day off," he said as he followed Janet into her office.

"I'm fine, just a little upset about something," she said.

"Do you want to talk about it?"

"Not really. Besides, I can't, but I'll be fine."

"Well, if you ever need a shoulder or a friend to just sit back and listen, I'm always available," Theodore said.

"Thank you, but seriously, I'll be fine," Janet replied as she sat down and took out her cell phone.

"Okay, I'm having a briefing with the staff around 2 pm. You're welcome to sit in if you're around."

"No, I'm just going to relax in my office today, you got it."

Theodore nodded his head and walked out of the office, closing the door behind him. As soon as he left, Janet started going through her cell phone, deleting pictures and all the text messages between her and Lonnie. After Face had explained everything to her, Janet knew to erase everything on her cell phone and then destroy it.

CHAPTER 51

Montgomery County

1:28 PM...

The grey Honda Accord slowly pulled up into the driveway and parked. After another long night of undercover surveillance work, Ken was ready to relax. After he got out of his car, he took out his keys and went inside the house. Ken turned on the living room light and sat his briefcase down on a chair. When he walked into the kitchen, he turned on the light and couldn't believe his eyes. Standing there, pointing their guns at Ken's head, was Face and his cousin King. "Sit down, Mr. Nelson," Face told him.

Ken quickly did as he was told. Instantly, the sweat began to fall down his face. "You been doing your homework, I see, and so have I," Face said.

"Please, I'm sorry, I was just doing my job. I'm just a private investigator for the Livingston Real Estate firm," Ken mumbled in fear.

"No, no, no! You're a lot more than a P.I. You've been working with Mark Livingston, Carter Samuels, and Sergio Miller for some time now, and you're also a member of The Knights of Liberty," Face said.

Ken's eyes lit up when he heard that. "You know about the K.O.L?"

"Yes, and all the crooked members associated. Like I said, Mr. Nelson, I've been doing my homework as well."

"How did y'all find me?"

"I had one of my men place a tracking device on your car. So while you were watching and following all my people, we were watching and following you," Face said.

"Please, don't kill me! Please Face!" Face grabbed Ken by his shirt collar and said, "Come the fuck on, you're going with us!"

King started to dial a number on his cellphone, and someone answered on the first ring. "Bring the van around the back," he said. Ken was pushed out of a back door and rushed into a waiting black van. He sat there scared and terrified as Face sat right across from him.

"So, Mr. Nelson, I found out that you don't like dogs," Face said.

"Why does that matter?" Ken stuttered. Face looked deep into Ken's terrified eyes and said, "I was told by my mother a long time ago. That we should always face our fears."

"Please, I'll give you whatever you want!" Ken said as the van drove away.

"I already have everything I need!" Face told him with a smirk.

CHAPTER 52

Downtown Philly

After their lunch meeting, Mark and Carter headed back over to the office. While inside the car, they were talking about Face. "Do you really think it will work, Carter?"

"I do. All we need is an official signature from Face, and I can have my people doctor up the paperwork to make it appear that Face was "negotiating" with you to sell his company. You would have to get rid of his entire family so there won't be any heirs around that will benefit from his death."

"That won't be hard at all. It's not like we've never done it before. There haven't been any word yet about his wife and children, but I'll have Ken get on it ASAP to find out where they are," Mark said.

"I saw the news yesterday; his driver was shot and killed, and another one of his men got shot as well," Carter said as the car pulled up in front of the building and parked.

"Yeah, we just missed him!" Mark replied.

"Well, that was a good thing you did."

"And why's that?"

"Because we still need Face's signature. Him being dead right now won't make sense."

"Damn, you're right! And I want that company. I'll have Sergio put something together. Face needs to get kidnapped so I can get his signature. Then I'll personally put the bullet in his head," Mark smiled.

"How's things going with the singer? Did you add her to your list yet?" Carter said, changing the subject.

"Not yet. The little bitch is playing hard to get, but I will soon, and when I do, I'm gonna treat her dirty like the little whore she is," Mark replied.

"She does have some nice songs," Carter said as they both stepped out of the car. "I just hope she has a nice ass and mouth!" Mark replied.

Quincy and Sosa were standing in front of Lonnie while he was tied up to a wooden chair. Lonnie had tried his best to talk himself out of sure death, but his words fell on deaf ears. He was a man who had worked for the enemy, so that made him an enemy, Quincy thought to himself. As they all waited inside this secret getaway home that belonged to Mark, Quincy checked his vibrating cell phone. It was a text from Face that read: We got the P.I: With a smile on his face, Quincy looked at Sosa and said, "Ken is dog food."

CHAPTER 53

North Philadelphia

Inside an old abandoned building near 20th & Allegheny Avenue, King pushed Ken to the floor and told him to get undressed. Also, inside the building were two of Face's men standing around holding guns. After Ken was totally naked, he lay there shivering on the cold floor. He had no idea what was going to happen to him.

One of the men walked over and placed handcuffs on Ken. "What's...what's...going on?" he stuttered. Moments later, Face walked into the room. Right beside him were his two rottweilers, Michael Angelo and Gabriel. Neither dog had been fed in three days. They both began to growl as thick saliva dropped from their mouths.

"Please! Please! Just shoot me!!" Ken screamed. "I have an envelope at my house with all the information and locations you need. I can give it to you; just don't kill me!" Ken said as he began to squirm on the floor. Face went inside his jacket and pulled out a thick white envelope. "You mean this envelope?" he said, waving it in the air.

Face looked down at his two hungry dogs and said, "Go, Eat!" The two rottweilers rushed towards Ken's naked body and started biting hard into his unprotected flesh. Instantly, blood, bones, and pieces of flesh started splattering all over the walls and floors. Ken's screams filled the entire room, but no one showed any type of emotion. They all just stood there watching as Ken was being eaten alive.

Moments later, Ken slumped to the floor, and his screams stopped. Surrounded by flesh, blood, and brain matter, the two dogs continued to eat his flesh. Finally, with a look of satisfaction in his eye, Face called the dogs off. "Let's go; we got other business to take care of," he said as they all walked out of the room. Laying there inside a large puddle of blood and bones was Ken Nelson's mangled corpse. His days and nights of watching others had come to a terrible end.

CHAPTER 54

Ardmore, PA

"I'll see you and that beautiful wife of yours tomorrow night at the lodge gathering," Senator Edward Preston said on the phone to Sam Livingston.

"I can't wait. Been waiting all year for our annual celebration party," Sam replied.

"Me as well; we have a lot of important things to discuss. Plus, we have a few new recruits I have to introduce you to."

"The wife and I are both excited, so we'll be sure to wear our finest clothes. Talk to you soon," Sam said before hanging up. Sam looked over at his wife and said, "Edward said that we have some new recruits. The Knights are getting bigger by the day. I'm really happy for the direction he's taking us."

"Yes, we all are. I'm about to call to get my hair and nails done. I want to look good tomorrow," Margaret said, standing up and walking upstairs.

West Philly...

Doc sat around in his basement with a menacing smile on his pale white face. He had just gotten a phone call from Face. So Doc knew exactly what that meant. Someone would be getting dropped off soon. Inside the dimly lit basement, Doc was surrounded by computers, monitors, surgical equipment, and two large gurneys. Doc looked over at the wall and saw his wife Marabella chained to it. She had been his hostage for over ten years. Before Doc made Marabella one of his many victims, he was a well-known lawyer named Peter J. Greenberg.

Once he was in Doc's captivity, he was transformed into a full fledge woman with new breasts, ass implants and a brand-new vagina. Then Doc made the former lawyer his wife and kept him chained inside the basement. He had also removed Peter's tongues so he could never speak. Doc was a twisted, homicidal, and homosexual serial killer. Since the early 90's, he had strangled, killed, and savagely beaten over two hundred men and women. Doc stood up and walked over to Marabella. Then he kneeled down beside her and began to run his hand through her hair.

"You'll be joined by a new sister wife soon, my love. Very, very soon," Doc smirked.

CHAPTER 55

Northeast Philadelphia

5:58 PM...

Quincy and Sosa watched from a living room window as the tinted black Ford pickup pulled into the driveway and parked. The car door opened, and a large, muscular white man got out and casually walked towards the front door. As soon as he walked into the house, he was quickly greeted with Quincy's .45 caliber on his head.

"Don't do or try nothing stupid, Sergio!" he told him. "Now, just take a seat." Sergio, completely caught off guard, did as he was told. Still, his mind was racing with thoughts of how he could get out of this current situation.

Suddenly, Lonnie was pushed into the room by Sosa and another armed man. "Go sit down next to your boss!" Sosa said. Sergio looked at Lonnie with a disgusted look on his face. He felt totally betrayed, and if he could, he would reach over and strangle Lonnie with his bare hands. "You fuck'n snake!"

"I'm sorry, boss, but they made me!" Lonnie cried out.

"Both of y'all shut the fuck up!" Quincy yelled out.

"Check this nigga!" Sosa said to his armed man. The man went over and checked Sergio. He found a small gun in his ankle holster and gave it to Sosa. As they all sat and stood around, the front door opened, and Face walked inside. He walked over to Sergio and stared deep into his eyes. "So, you're the infamous Sergio Miller. The man with over two hundred kills. The man who shot my friend right over there and who sent a hitman to murder my entire family. And Mark Livingston's right-hand man and personal assassin."

"So you did your homework, I see; good job, Face. Because I know all about you as well," Sergio replied. Face went into his pocket and took out a long, sharp switchblade. "Unlike you, I'm a man of principles and honor, but I hate two types of people: snitches and pedophiles," Face said as he tossed Sergio the knife. "You already know what it is, so I'm going to let you handle your business before I handle mine.

Lonnie sat there with a confused look on his face. As soon as he began to speak, Sergio started to stab him repeatedly in the throat and chest. The blood from Lonnie's neck squirted all over the sofa. In a rush of pure rage, Sergio continued to stab Lonnie's body until his mangled corpse slumped down the sofa. He then looked up at Face and smiled. Blood was covered all over his hands and clothes.

Sergio then placed the knife down on the floor with a look of evil in his eyes. He calmly said, "Okay, thank you for that; now you can handle your business," he said, closing his eyes. With his loaded .45 gripped in his hand, Quincy walked over to Sergio, pointed his gun at his head, and pulled the trigger. Blowing a huge piece of Sergio's brain all over Lonnie's dead body.

"Make sure you get his cell phone out of the truck," Face said to Sosa.

"Okay, I'm on it," Sosa said as he walked out of the house. Face looked at Quincy and said, "You feel better?"

"A lot better; that son of a bitch shot me and killed my man," Quincy replied with a smile.

"Two down; now it's time to get all the bigger fish," Face said before they all left the house.

Wilmington, Delaware...

Gotti and one of his men back up the black van into the wide driveway of the DuPont Chemical plant. Standing right outside was a group of uniformed workers carrying barrels and boxes filled with C-4 and T.N.T. explosives. After the man loaded up the van and closed the doors, Gotti passed a thick white envelope to one of the men. Then he rolled up the window and drove away. He was headed back to Philly to go see Face and Quincy. As the van headed back down I-95, the sounds of Tupac's *All Eyes on Me,* flowed out the window.

CHAPTER 56

Early the next day...

Tucked inside a luxurious Airbnb near Penn Landing, Carter Samuels was tied down to a large king-size bed with long black leather straps. Standing right over him was a large, muscular, naked black man. The man had just finished performing anal sex on Carter. The man walked over and grabbed his cell phone from a table. He looked over at Carter, who was now completely drained from their all-night sex session. He started dialing a number and a man's voice answered on the first ring. "He's all yours," the man said before ending the call.

The man then started to get dressed. After he put back on all his clothes and shoes, he grabbed an envelope full of cash from off the table and walked out of the bedroom. Marvin had been tracking Carter's every move for the past week. Carter had no idea that his black lover had double-crossed him for a large sum of money. As Carter lay there still feeling drained and fatigued, Face and Quincy walked into the room. The disgusting sight of a short, fat, old, naked white man strapped to a bed was hard to watch. Face sat down beside Carter and smacked him in the face. Carter quickly looked up and was in complete shock at the face looking right at him.

"Hey, Mr. Samuels, surprised to see me?"

"Oh shit! How did you find me? Please, it was all Mark's plan, he wants your company. He wants your family dead! Please, Face, I can be an asset to you if you spare my life. I know Mark's entire business. I can sign off on any and everything. I'm his official lawyer and the only person with permission to sign off on his name. Just don't kill me. I have a wife and kids!" Carter cried out.

Face looked down at the frightened man and said, "Okay, Mr. Samuels, but if you want to walk out of here alive, first I'm gonna need you to call Mark and tell 'em everything I say," Face replied.

"I'll do it! Just promise me that you won't kill me."

"I won't if you do as I say," Face said.

After Quincy untied Carter from the leather straps, he passed him his cell phone. Face told him what to say, and Carter called Mark on his personal cellphone. "Hey Carter, what's going on?" Mark said as he pushed the naked woman beside him away. "I won't be in the office today. I'm feeling a little under the weather."

"Okay, get you some rest. Will you be able to make it to the lodge meeting tonight? It's the anniversary party."

"I'm not sure, but you know if I can, I'll be there," Carter said. "Also, I talked with Sergio last night, and he said that he was going out of town to do a job."

"Why didn't he just call me? He usually does, but okay, I'll wait for him to call me," Mark said.

"Are you okay, Carter? You sound a little off."

"I'm fine, like I said, just feeling a little under the weather."

"Okay, get well. I'll talk to you later," Mark said before ending the call. Face looked at Carter and said, "Good job. Now, I need a much bigger favor from you."

"Anything, you name it, and it's done," Carter said as he began to put back on his clothes.

"I had my lawyers put together some paperwork and other legal documents. I also know that you and Mark both control all the company funds on the four offshore accounts that y'all opened a few years back. I had my people thoroughly go through all the company's records, files, and other important documents. I'm gonna need you to access all of those funds and transfer them into another offshore account in the Caymans."

"I can't access the passcodes without Mark's help. I only have the first four numbers, and he has the last four. That's the only way we can authorize a large transfer of money from one bank to another," Carter said.

"Okay, fine. Mark will be joining you soon," Face said.

CHAPTER 57

Ardmore, Pa

Sam and Margaret Livingston had no idea that they were being watched and followed. After going to the car wash and supermarket, they got inside their Cadillac SUV and headed back to their beautiful, secluded home. They were both excited about the Knights of Liberty anniversary party and meeting the new members.

Hidden inside their home, Gotti and two of his men were waiting patiently. They had been there for the past hour. Marvin had managed to deactivate the security alarm system, giving them access to the home. They had driven there in an ambulance and parked it a few blocks away from the home. The silver Cadillac pulled into the driveway and parked. Sam and Margaret both got out carrying grocery bags. They had no idea that they were about right into a life-changing situation.

Santa, Marta Colombia...

Tasha sat back in a long beach chair, watching as her children were jumping in and out of the large Olympic-sized pool. They were both playing with Carlos and his three children. As she sat there smiling and enjoying the beaming hot sun, her cell phone started ringing. "Hello," she quickly answered with excitement.

"Hey, Queen, are you and the kids having fun?" Face asked.

"Too much fun! It's a new adventure every day around here," Tasha replied. "Are you good in Philly?"

"Yes, everything is going well, and I will be sending for y'all very soon. I miss my family," Face replied.

"And we definitely miss our Daddy," Tasha said with a smile.

"I have to take this call right now, babe. I'll call you back later tonight," Face said.

"Okay, Daddy, I'll be in bed waiting to hear your voice," Tasha said before hanging up.

"Wassup?" Face said, answering the other line.

"We got the parents," Gotti said.

"They're both tied up inside the ambulance. Marvin was able to deactivate the alarm system, and everything went smooth."

"Okay, perfect, take them to the house and have a few of your men stay there with them until we get there," Face said.

"Will do. I just hope the old man don't have a heart attack on me. He fainted twice," Gotti laughed.

"What about his wife?"

"She a lot tougher than his old ass. I had to duct tape her mouth to stop getting cursed out," he laughed.

CHAPTER 58

Laurel Hill Cemetery

That Evening...

Jerome Kinsley and his four-man crew of cemetery workers were hard at work. Face paid Jerome to dig up five plots at the far end of the cemetery. Since Jerome and Face had been working together, over seventy-five bodies had been buried there. Each one of them had met their demise by crossing Face.

New York City...

Frank "Underworld" Simms sat down at the large conference table, looking at his gold Rolex watch. He was at an important record executive meeting with the heads of his A&R department. While one of the executives was discussing some new marketing and promotional strategies, Frank started texting on his cellphone. After the meeting was over, Frank rushed out the building and had one of his men drive him back to Philly.

Inside a small row home near 42nd and Mantua, Marvin had all his computer software set up and ready to go. He then looked over at the three scared people who were tied and duct-taped to wooden chairs. Carter Samuels, Sam, and Margaret

Livingston each had terrified looks on their pale white faces. Marvin had gotten all the codes, paperwork, and passwords from Carter to make a large money transfer from one offshore account to another. The only thing he needed to complete the final transfer was the last four numbers from Mark. Standing around were two armed men dressed in black, waiting for orders from Face.

Washington, D.C...

Leo Renolds and U.S. Senator Edward Preston sat back inside the black Cadillac SUV headed toward Philadelphia. That night was the anniversary party for the Knights of Liberty. Neither one would dare miss it. There was a long list of very important and influential people that were going to be at the event tonight. Two four-star Generals, six members from the United Nations, five Governors, and the heads of all the major national news media outlets: CNN, FOX, Disney, and so many others.

"Looking forward to tonight?" Leo asked.

"Sure am. I have so much to talk about. The first issue is discussing more ways to get Blacks and Spanish off the streets and more of those people incarcerated. I'm suggesting a few new laws get passed," Edward said.

CHAPTER 59

Downtown Philadelphia

Inside his luxurious condominium...

Mark stood in front of a large mirror, admiring himself. For many people, he was considered a vein, spoiled rich boy. He had never once needed anything because it was always given to him by his wealthy parents. Being tall, dark, and handsome, Mark was used to women throwing themselves at him and men fearing him. His ultimate goal in life was to become the wealthiest and most powerful man in the entire U.S.

He admired people like the Rothschilds, Vanderbilts, and Waltons, as well as his good friends Elon Musk and Bill Gates. His ideology was that the rich and wealthy should run and control the entire world and eliminate the poor. As Mark stood in front of the mirror fixing his tuxedo, his cell phone started to ring. "Hey, Edward," he answered.

"Mark, I'm with Leo right now, and we're headed to Philly for the anniversary party tonight," Edward said.

"I'll be there for sure. I'm actually getting myself together now," Mark replied.

"Will Carter and Sergio be there?"

"Yes, I'm sure they will be there. They're loyal members of the movement. Carter's not feeling too good, but he won't miss it, and Sergio is out of town right now on a job," Mark said.

"Okay, then I'll see you later tonight," Edward said before ending the call.

As soon as Edward ended the call, Mark's phone started ringing again. When Mark saw who was calling him, his blue eyes lit up. "Hello, beautiful," he answered.

"Hey, handsome, I was lying back in my bed, and you crossed my mind. Honestly, I've been thinking about you a lot lately," Ashley Jay said in a soft, seductive voice.

"So, what do you have in mind?" Mark asked as he walked over and sat down on a sofa.

"I was thinking that maybe you can come over to my Penthouse and have a glass of wine with me."

"Well, I do have an event I'm getting ready for, but I don't see a problem with coming by for a few."

"Okay, I'll text you my address. See you soon, Mark," Ashley said before the call ended. Mark sat there with a big smile on his face. Ashley Jay was the one woman he had yet to sleep with. With a look of lust in his eyes, Mark grabbed his car keys and rushed out the door.

CHAPTER 60

Downtown Philly

Janet walked down the hallway and entered Theodore's office. She closed the door and sat down in an empty chair. "Face wanted to thank you for putting all the paperwork together. He's been very busy lately, but he asked me to tell you that all your work has been appreciated", Janet said.

"It's not a problem at all. I'm very grateful to have been given another chance and to once again feel appreciated," Theodore replied as he shut down and closed his laptop. "But I am a little curious. Why would Face need paperwork to purchase other companies without first doing the proper research? One of two things could happen: either he has discovered the business deal of the century, or he will lose a ton of money."

Janet looked over at Theodore and said, "Face always knows what he's doing. What may seem like a flaw to others is like perfection to Face. In time, you'll see for yourself. He plays the game of chess, so every move he makes is calculated," Janet said as she stood up to leave.

"I believe you; I really do. There have been a lot of rumors about Face around this city. Some good, some bad, but none foolish," Theodore said.

Ardmore, PA...

Lodge #5 was located in a secluded, wooden area away from all the locals. Hidden behind tall trees and high bushes, Gotti and six of his most loyal men had just secretly placed the C-4 and TNT explosives all around the large property. Next to Gotti was a small detonator that was built by Marvin. Dressed in camouflage, Gotti and his crew watched as the swarm of luxury vehicles arrived and parked one by one.

They were all members of the Knights of Liberty secret society. Neither of them knew that the building had been rigged with enough explosives to blow up a small town. Dressed in tuxedos and long gowns, there were lots of smiles, hugs, and handshakes by the members. Gotti sat there, looking through a pair of black binoculars. The anger and hate he had for these people was boiling inside his soul. Gotti looked at his Tag Heuer watch and sat there waiting, but his patience was running thin.

CHAPTER 61

The Rittenhouse condominium was one of the most expensive buildings in all of Philly. It had a market value of 20 million. Built in 2017, it had over 900 square feet of space. When Mark arrived, Ashley buzzed him in through a private door that wasn't monitored by any of the cameras. Laying across the sofa, Ashley had on an all-white silk nightgown. Her long black hair fell down her back, and she smelled like a bottle of Les Larmes Sacrees de Thebes perfume.

On the glass table was a bottle of Moet & Chandon, Dom Perignon Champagne. The door opened, and Mark walked inside. He was a little stunned by the elegance of the home. A large chandelier and fine art gave the place a touch of pure wealth. Mark walked over while Ashley was pouring them both a glass of champagne. He sat next to her and gave her a hug and a soft kiss on the lips.

"This is very nice," Mark said as he perused the layout of the home.

"Thank you, Hun. I'm glad you like it; let me know if you ever need a home decorator. My girl is the best," Ashley said as she passed Mark a glass of champagne.

"Let's toast," Ashley said. Mark smiled as he couldn't keep his eyes off of Ashley's firm round breast, perking through her nightgown.

"Here's to a bright future and lots of fun," Ashley said.

"Yes, to lots of fun," Mark said before sipping on his champagne. After the toast, Ashley moved over and placed her arms around Mark's neck. She could see the hardness inside his pants growing. She kissed Mark softly on the neck and whispered in his ears, "I can't wait to suck that big cock." Mark sat there feeling dizzy and tried to shake it off.

"You...you drug...me," Mark slurred out before finally dozing off.

The GHB (gamma-hydroxybutyric acid), Ketamine, and Rohypnol were the most popular date-rape drugs on the market. It was the same drug that Mark had used on unsuspected women when he was back in college.

Ashley watched as the three large men carried Mark's body over to a waiting ambulance. It was one of the three ambulances that Face had owned. The three men were each dressed in blue paramedic uniforms, but neither of them knew anything about the medical field. They were all loyal street soldiers on Face's payroll.

After seeing the men place Mark's body into the ambulance, Ashley walked back inside her home and started to wipe down all the door knobs and glasses on the table. She didn't want any indication that Mark had been there. She had already placed his cell phone inside a Ziploc bag, but not before deleting any of their recent text messages. Ashley grabbed her cell phone and quickly made a call. "Hello," Frank answered.

"It's done; he's on his way to the next location," she said.

"Thanks, Ashley, I'm proud of you."

"Like I said, there's nothing in this world I wouldn't do for you."

"Ditto," Frank said before ending the call.

Edward Preston looked at his rearview mirror and noticed the lights of the blue and white Philadelphia police car behind him. He pulled over to the side of the road and watched as the two officers got out of their patrol car.

"How can I help you, officer?" Edward asked in a frustrated tone.

"A vehicle fitting this car was just reported stolen by two white men," the officer said.

"Do you know who the hell I am?" Edward said as he, too, got out of the car in a rage. The two officers quickly pulled out their guns and ordered both men to place their hands in the air.

"The hell I will!" Leo shouted. "I will have both of y'all assholes on desk duty for the next 20 years!' he said.

"We're just doing our job, sir," the officer said as he pushed both men into the car and handcuffed them both. "I'm a US Senator, and this is my car!" Edward shouted.

"We're going to run it in, and we should find out soon," the officer said.

"I'm going to need y'all to sit in the back of the patrol car while we check your IDs," the officer said.

"I'll have y'all jobs for this!" Leo said as he was being shoved into the back of the patrol car. The two officers quickly got back into the car and slammed the doors. Then, one of the officers looked back, aiming his gun at Edward and Leo. They watched as he took out a cell phone and made a call. "Hello," Face answered.

"We got them; now we're headed to the house," the officer said.

"Good job, Nate, I'll make sure you and Vince get a bonus for this one," Face said before ending the call.

"Are y'all fools kidnapping us?" Edward asked in a surprised voice.

"You can't kidnap a US Senator and the United States Attorney General!"

"Well, we just did, and to be honest, we don't care anything about y'all flamboyant titles. Save that crap for the people in Washington, DC. Right now, y'all are in Philly, and Philly doesn't give a fuck!" Nate said.

Edward and Leo both sat back in total shock. They couldn't believe what was happening or who was behind their kidnapping. Nate leaned back and took away their cell phones. The entire time, he kept his gun pointed at their heads.

"Whatever y'all two are being paid, I'll double it. I can have the money sent to your accounts in less than an hour," Edward said.

"Just give up a number," Leo said.

Both Vince and Nate started laughing. Edward and Leo both had bemused looks on their faces. "Okay, I'll triple it," Edward said. He was sure that his money could change their minds. As the patrol car swerved through the Philly traffic, moments later, the car pulled up and parked outside of a West Philly rowhome. "What will it be?" Edward said as fear began to sweep throughout his body. Nate looked deep into Edward's eyes and said, "Mr. Senator and Mr. U.S. Attorney, y'all don't have enough money to pay us to turn on our boss."

"Who is your boss?" Leo asked.

"His name is Face," Vince told them.

CHAPTER 62

West Philadelphia

Cityline Avenue...

Face looked over at Quincy with a big smile on his face. "We got them all! Every last one of them," he said with excitement.

"They really misjudged you, and it cost them. Mark had no idea about the man he chose to go to war with," Quincy replied as his car turned down Belmont Avenue.

"Not a clue, and now we are about to find out what it is that Mark loves more: money, power, family, or his life," Face said.

"I called the house and had Carter and his parents taken over to Doc's house like you asked. Marvin will be there too," Quincy said.

"Good, I want this done and over with. I miss my family, and I'm ready to bring them back home," Face said.

Over five hundred people had showed up for the Knights of Liberty anniversary party. Gotti watched from a short distance until the final person walked through the door. Everyone inside the building was conversing and enjoying the festivities. All patiently waited for Edward, Mark, and a few others to show up. It wasn't like them to be late, especially for an event with so much importance.

As the boisterous crowd continued on, Gotti had one of his men run up and place a thick chain around the front door handle. He also had his men chain-lock all the other doors to prevent any escape. Now, no one could get out of the building. The people inside didn't have a clue that they were now all trapped like caged animals at the zoo. As Gotti sat there holding the small detonator, he felt the vibration from his cell phone.

When he looked at his cell phone, he saw the text from Face: BURN THE HATE: the text message read. Gotti pressed a red button on the detonator, and the entire building exploded, sending a mushroom of fire into the dark sky. A black cloud of fire and debris hovered over lodge #5. The screams and cries could be heard coming from all the dying attendees. Trapped inside a burning inferno of wood and brick, all the people inside were being cooked alive. Gotti and his crew quickly got into a waiting van and drove away as the sounds of fire trucks and police sirens were getting louder.

CHAPTER 63

West Philly

Face entered into the small rowhome with King and Quincy by his side. When he walked down into the basement, he saw Edward and Lee both tied up to wooden chairs. The fear in both men's eyes was evident as the smell of fear filled the room. Face stood in front of them with a serious look on his face. "Do y'all know who I am?" Both men nodded their heads with a yes. "Then, I'm sure y'all know about my reputation," he asked.

"What is it you want, Face?" Edward asked. "Just tell us, and it's done, but please don't let me die like this!" he added.

"Like what? Like all the Blacks and Hispanics in the ghetto? Like all the poor and unfortunate who die every day on the streets from y'all gun and drug laws! You mean you don't want to die like my people? US Citizens that are dying and being taken advantage of every single day by the rich and wealthy," Face fumed. "I know who both of y'all are and everything y'all stand for. White supremacy and power, and I also know everything about the Knights of Liberty and y'all agenda. The hate y'all have for every race on Earth that's not white."

"Look, Face; I'm the US Attorney General, for god's sake. If you kill us, do you really think you would get away with it? The US government will search and turn over every rock to find out who is responsible! We are not one of your drug enemies; he is a US Senator, and I'm the top law enforcer in the country, so maybe you need to think this out more," Leo said.

Face laughed and said, "Did they find out who murdered Senator C.W. Watson or all the members of the COUP?

"That was you?" Edward asked in shock.

"That was me! All of me!" Face said as he looked over at King and nodded his head. King pulled up two loaded .9mm and approached the two men. "Any final words?" Face asked.

"Fuck you!" Leo said.

"Please! Please don't let me die like this!" Edward cried out.

Aiming the guns at Edward and Leo's heads, King pulled the triggers, unloading a round of bullets in both men's heads and bodies. Face watched as the two men slumped dead in their chairs.

"Have your men take the bodies to the cemetery; Jerome is waiting," Face told King. Then he and Quincy left and headed over to Doc's house.

CHAPTER 64

Laurel Hill Cemetery

Twenty minutes later...

Jerome watched as the black van backed up into the cemetery. When the back doors opened, he saw the two dead, naked bodies inside. King had his men burn all of their clothes and belongings to destroy any evidence that would lead back to them. Jerome watched as his men grabbed the naked bodies and then tossed them both into a pre-made grave.

"Two down and three more to go," Jerome said as he stood there smoking a cigar.

North Philadelphia...

Sitting down inside his large, opulent living room, Sosa was surrounded by trusted members of his crew. They were all tuned into CNN. On the large 65-inch Sony TV was the biggest story of the day, about the explosion of Lodge #5, right on the outskirts of Philadelphia. The news reporter said that there were no survivors and at least 300 people had died.

Sosa grabbed the remote control and switched to FOX News. It was the same story on every channel. Investigators and CSI agents were still trying to figure out what had happened. Sosa sat back with a smile on his face. Deep down, he was very impressed by the genius of Face. Knowing that Face was a true master of war.

Frank "Underworld" Simms was being driven by one of his men when he heard the voice on the radio talking about the massive explosion near Philadelphia. Sitting next to him was his superstar pop artist, Ashley Jay. She didn't have a single clue why Frank suddenly started smiling. "What so funny?"

"Oh, nothing," Frank replied.

"Oh, it's something, but whatever it is, you're very excited about it," Ashley said as the driver slowly pulled up and parked in front of the Ritz Carlton Hotel. They were going to a pre-grammy party that Ashley was hosting.

"One day, you're going to have to tell me what's so damn funny," she said as the driver opened the door.

"I'm sorry, Queen, but somethings ain't meant to ever be told. And this is one that I'm going to take to my grave with me," Frank said as he followed behind Ashley into the waiting press and red carpet.

CHAPTER 65

West Philly

Inside Doc's dimly lit basement, Carter, Sam, and his wife Margaret were all seated in chairs. Fear was in each of their blue eyes. Also inside the basement was Marvin, holding his laptop, and three of Face's armed men. Locked and chained on a wall was Mark Livingston. He was still half out of it from the effects of the drugs he had taken. Standing right in front of him was Doc. Staring hard and licking his lips with pure lust in his eyes.

Before chaining Mark to his wall of horror, Doc had undressed him. Now, Mark's fully naked body was on display. Chained on a nearby wall was Doc's wife, Marabella. Carter, Sam, and Margaret didn't have a clue what was going to happen to them. Suddenly, the door opened, and Face and Quincy walked down the stairs into the basement. Quincy was holding a notebook and three black markers.

Face approached Mark's chained, naked body and splashed a cold bottle of spring water on his face. Everyone watched as Mark slowly started to come to his senses. "Get me another water," Face told one of his men.

One of the men rushed over to a table and got another cold bottle of water, passing it to Face. Face splashed the second bottle over Mark's head. Mark quickly awakened from his daze and looked around the room at all the different faces.

"What the hell is going on? Dad, Mom, Carter, what's going on?" he yelled out.

"Who the fuck are you?" he asked Doc.

"Your future husband," Doc said with a menacing grin. Mark then looked over at Face and just shook his head. Right then he knew that he was in some deep trouble.

"Please! Please! Face, let me make up for all the trouble I caused you and your family! Please just give me a number, and it's all yours," Mark begged.

Face looked at Mark and said, "Right now, all I need from you is the last 4-digits to your offshore accounts. I got the first four from Carter."

"There's over two billion dollars in those accounts!" Mark said.

"Does it matter if you and your family aren't around to enjoy it?" Face said. "Now, what's the goddamn numbers!"

Mark looked around at the situation he was in and knew that Face had the upper hand. Seeing his parents and Carter all tied down to the chairs, he decided to give Face the final four numbers to the offshore bank accounts.

"7249," Mark said. Already prepared and ready to make the transfers, Marvin typed in the last four numbers and watched as all the funds from Mark's bank were being transferred to another offshore bank account that Face had set up. In less than five minutes, over 2.3 billion dollars from

Mark's offshore accounts had been emptied out and was now in Face account.

"So, this is what it's all about? Money?" Mark said.

"No, it's about so much more, Mark! So much more," Face replied.

"What is it, Face, that you want? You have me and my parents locked down inside this dungeon. Now you have the money, so what else do you want from me?"

Face looked deep into Mark's scared eyes and said, "Everything!" Quincy walked over and passed Mark a piece of paper and a pen.

"Read carefully and sign the document," Face told him. Mark perused through the paper and shook his head in disbelief.

"You want twenty of my companies? Are you fucking serious? My money, my companies!" Mark said. "I'm not signing this! They are all companies I earned and built!" Mark said.

Face looked at Mark with evil eyes and said, "You lying no good son of a bitch! They are all the companies you stole or forced people to give or sell to you! You didn't earn shit! You're a business bully and criminal, Mark Livingston!"

"I'm not signing that document!" Mark shouted. Face looked at Quincy and nodded his head. Then Quincy pulled out his loaded .45, walked over to Carter, and aimed the gun at his head. "Please, Mark, just sign the damn paper! Please!"

Before Mark could say another word, Quincy pulled the trigger, blowing a portion of Carter's brain on Sam Livingston's shirt. Everyone watched as Carter's dead corpse slumped down in the chair. The sight of seeing Carter's brain blowing out made Margaret throw up.

"This is the last time that I'm going to ask you to sign the papers!" Face told Mark. Mark looked at his scared, crying parents and decided to sign the papers. He had just relinquished all ownership to twenty real estate businesses and a few beach properties.

"You won, Face! Now can me and my parents leave! I don't have nothing more to give you."

"I have one more thing to tell you," Face said.

"What! What! And can you please tell this crazy man to stop staring at me!" Mark yelled.

Doc looked at Mark and just smiled. "What is it that you have to tell me?"

"That all your friends are now dead. Edward Preston, Leo Renolds, Sergio Miller, Ken Nelson, and now your lawyer, Carter Samuels. Only you and your parents are still alive, but only one of y'all will be spared tonight," Face said.

"You killed them all?"

"Every last one of them! And every single member of your Knights of Liberty society. So, like I said, right now it's three of y'all left, but only one will survive sure death; I'll let y'all three decide," Face said as he watched Quincy walk over and pass a piece of paper and a small black marker to Sam and Margaret. Quincy then took the signed document from Mark and gave him a marker and a piece of paper.

"What's this for?"

"I want each of y'all to write down the names of two people that should die here tonight. Like I said, only one person will survive," Face said.

"Are you serious?" Mark said.

"Dead ass!" Face replied in a serious tone. "Now, start writing!"

Doc stood back, watching it all. This was the most excitement he had in years.

"Just do it, son," Sam yelled out. Mark watched as his parent began to write on the papers. Then he started writing as well. "Are y'all done?"

"Yes, we are done," Sam said. Face walked over and took the pieces of paper from everyone. Then he looked at each one of them. He read Sam's first, "My son should live, take my wife and me." Then he read Margaret's, "Take me and my husband, save our son." Face then walked over to Mark and read his paper, "Take my parents!"

Face looked deep into Mark's eyes and said, "So fear is stronger than love."

Quincy then walked over to Sam and Margaret and shot them both in the head. They both died instantly, just a few feet away from Carter Samuel.

Mark couldn't believe it. He was lost in a world of pain, confusion, and anger. A flow of tears fell from his blue eyes. Thoughts of one day getting his revenge roamed through his head. He would do and say anything to stay alive. Everything and everyone he had loved was now gone, and the man standing right in front of him was responsible. He didn't know what Face was going to do with him now.

Face had the upper hand and was the puppet master of it all. Face had all the aces, and Mark had none. It was a situation that he could have never imagined being in. He was always the alpha male, imposing his dominance on all the weak and less fortunate. He was the King on the chessboard who controlled the what, where, when, and why people did what he demanded. For the first time in his life, Mark felt he had met his match. Not just a chess player but a grandmaster.

"So, Ashley Jay was a part of it all?" Mark asked as he remembered her being the last person he was with.

"I'm sure you know that by now," Face said.

"Can I just ask you; how did you pull all of this off?"

"We placed a GPS tracker on your private investigator, Ken. He gave us all the locations where you and your friends visit and hang out. Then the rest was easy," Face replied. Mark just shook his head, disappointed in himself for not being more meticulous and prepared!

"So, are you going to spare my life like you promised me? Or was that a lie?"

"Ye, I'm going to keep my word, Mark. I have everything I need now; you're no longer my responsibility. You're his," Face said, pointing at Doc. Face told his men to carry the bodies of Carter, Sam, and Margaret out the back door to a waiting ambulance. Marvin grabbed his laptop and followed them out.

"What do you mean I'm his responsibility?" Mark asked with a confused look on his face.

As Mark stood locked and chained to the concrete wall, Doc approached him, showing a row of rotten brown teeth, and said, "You heard the boss, Annabella; you're all my responsibility now."

"Anabella!" Mark replied.

"Yes, from this moment on, that's your new name," Doc said as he pulled out a large syringe. Mark looked around the basement and saw that a naked woman was chained to a wall. The woman began to act hysterical and out of control. Moaning and grunting in a speech that only Doc understood.

"Calm down, Marabella, you're going to eat soon. Are you happy to have a new friend?" Doc asked her. When she began to grunt louder, Mark noticed that the woman didn't have a tongue. It had been removed many years earlier.

"Face, what is this? Please don't leave me here with this maniac and that crazy woman," Mark yelled out.

Face looked over at Mark and said, "Do you remember a well-known lawyer by the name of Peter J. Greenberg?"

"Yes, I remember Peter. He worked with Carter, and we did some work together before he disappeared a few years ago; why do you ask?"

Face pointed to the woman chained in the corner and said, "Look very closely, Mark. Do you see any resemblance? That's your friend Peter over there!"

"What! Are you serious?"

"He's been here a very long time, now married to my good friend Doc, and now you will be joining him," Face said as he and Quincy started walking up the stairs.

"Face! Face! Please just kill me! Please come back! Don't do this to me! Please!" Mark screamed out. Then, in one quick motion, Doc stabbed Mark in the neck with the syringe and stood there while began to slowly drift into a place of darkness. After Mark was totally unconscious, Doc unchained his naked body and dragged him over to a waiting gurney. With an evil grin on his face, Doc was ready to perform his male-to-female sex reassignment surgery.

Doc had studied and mastered vaginal construction (vaginoplasty). It was the same surgery he had performed on Peter J. Greenberg.

Sitting inside a black Mercedes Benz, Face and Qunicy were talking about all the day's events.

"It's all done, just like you planned, Face. They never knew what was coming."

"Most rich, cocky people never see the fall from grace until it's too late. They are too high-strung on their gold thrones to see that the servant who carries the food tray has poisoned the food. Not because of hate, but because of constant disrespect and humiliation," Face replied. "I was told by my mother to never look down on a man unless you're lending a hand to help him up," he added.

"Well, you definitely made Doc's day," Quincy laughed.

"Doc needs the company; he was dying to add a new wife to his stable," Face laughed.

Jerome watched as the ambulance backed up and the two doors opened. Once again, his men started to drag out the three dead corpses and throw them into the large pre-made graves. After all the bodies were placed into the ground, a small forklift began to cover them all with fresh dirt. Edward Preston, Carter Samuels, Leo Renold, Sam, and Margaret Livingston were all once high-ranking members of upper-class American society. With so many years of hate, greed, and betrayal amongst them, now they were nothing more than food for the worms.

Later that night...

Inside his beautiful furnished Chestnut Hill home, Face sat down on the sofa with a pleased look on his face. The war was finally over, and once again, he could breathe and not stay looking over his shoulder. It was a feeling that he could never get used to or would ever allow to happen again. He picked up his cell phone and called his lovely wife, Tasha. "Hello, my King, tell me some good news," she said.

"Carlos will be putting y'all on a plane to come back home tomorrow morning. I can't wait to see y'all, babe. I really miss my family."

"And we miss you too, Daddy," Tasha replied.

CHAPTER 66

Washington, DC, The White House

One week later...

Inside a large, private conference room, U.S. President Donald Winston was seated at the head of a large black oval table. He was surrounded by all the heads of the State Department and also the FBI, CIA, and NSA directors. Also, there was the newly assigned U.S. Attorney General, Calvin Humphrey.

"I want whoever is responsible brought to justice! I want goddamn answers! This is one of the most tragic events in U.S. history! Whoever is responsible will and must pay! What do you have so far, Attorney General?" The President fumed.

"At the present time, we have a short list of suspects that could've pulled something like this off," Calvin said. "The Chinese, The Russians, The Mexicans, and members of Al Qaeda, just to name a few. We also believe that North Korea could be involved. We lost two U.S. senators, our Attorney General, and so many others in that building. And we still have yet to find most of the bodies. I've received tips from informants, spies, and even Interpol about this situation, Mr. President. One name did come across my desk, but it's far fetch, and to be honest, I think it's a game or some type of prank."

"What name is that?" The President asked as he tilted his glasses to the tip of his nose.

"A man named Norman Smith Jr. from out of Philadelphia. He also goes by the street name Face," Calvin said.

"But like I said, that's a reach and more of a prank. Norman Smith Jr. is nothing more than a former drug boss who won a major drug trial some years ago and went legit. He is now a self-made billionaire after investing his money into real estate."

"Do you think he's worth looking into?" the President asked. After a long pause, Calvin said, "I'll have my people look, but I'm sure we won't find anything. Our focus needs to be on the Chinese. Before Leo had disappeared, he had two meetings with diplomats from the Chinese Embassy. I believe they are heavily involved with all of this. Also, there was a massacre of twenty Chinese crime figures in Philadelphia not too long ago, and I believe there's some type of connection. We learned from surveillance cameras that the Attorney General and Senator Preston got into a vehicle and drove down to Philadelphia."

"I want you to look under every rock and get down to the bottom of this! I'll schedule another meeting later in the week," the President said as he stood up and left the room.

EPILOGUE

Face had donated one billion dollars from the offshore accounts to over one hundred community-based non-profit organizations along the East Coast. Each donation was to help underprivileged boys and girls growing up in cruel, harsh environments. He also used a large sum of money to build affordable housing in Philly, Pittsburgh, Camden, NJ, Baltimore, Cleveland, Chicago, Detroit, New York, Boston, Miami, and other small towns throughout Pennsylvania. Face had also returned Theodore Robert's real estate company back to him. Face was now one of the biggest commercial real estate investors and stockholders in America. From the ghettos of West Philly to the very top of the American hierarchy, there would be no one else like Norman Smith Jr., Known simply as Black Scarface.

MUSIC BY JIMMY DASAINT

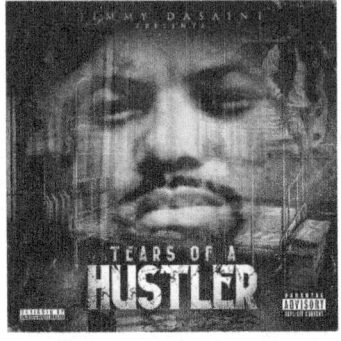

TEARS OF A HUSTLER

DIARY OF A HUSTLER

STILL A HUSTLER

AVAILABLE ON ALL STREAMING PLATFORMS

WE SHIP TO PRISONS

BLACK SCARFACE

BLACK SCARFACE II

BLACK SCARFACE III

BLACK SCARFACE IV

DOC

KING

KING 2

KILLADELPHIA

ON EVERYTHING I LOVE

MONEY DESIRES & REGRETS

WHAT EVERY WOMAN WANTS

YOUNG RICH & DANGEROUS

THE UNDERWORLD

A ROSE AMONG THORNS

A ROSE AMONG THORNS 2

SEX SLAVE

WE SHIP TO PRISONS

AIN'T NO SUNSHINE   WHO   THE DARKEST CORNER   HOTTEST SUMMER EVER

BLACK GOTTI   CONTRACT KILLER   THE 21 LESSONS OF LIFE   THE 21 LESSONS OF SUCCESS

SOSA   LEGEND   PLEASE DON'T TOUCH ME THERE

WE SHIP TO PRISONS

NEW RELEASES

BLACK SCARFACE 5

COMING SOON

THE DYNASTY EMPIRE
PART I

THE DYNASTY EMPIRE
PART II

WE SHIP TO PRISONS

DASAINT ENTERTAINMENT SPECIALS ✓
Orders being shipped to a **PRISON FACILITY ONLY**, qualify for the 3 for $40.00 Special! The books marked with a red checkmark can be purchased. This special **does not** include the BLACK SCARFACE Series, DOC, KING titles, The 21 Lessons of Life, SOSA or LEGEND. The flat rate shipping for these items is $10.00.

DASAINT ENTERTAINMENT REFUND POLICY
No Refunds Will Be Processed. All Sales Are Final!
If you submit the wrong address for any order or forget an inmate identification number, you must pay the shipping cost again, for those books to be redelivered.

If your item is returned to us by a prion facility, for any reason, you must pay to have those items shipped to another address. Return merchandize are held for ninety days. If they are not claimed by then, they will not be shipped out.

Fill out this form and send it to:
DASAINT ENTERTAINMENT
PO BOX 97
BALA CYNWYD, PA 19004

TITLE	PRICE	QTY
BLACK SCARFACE	$15.00	_____
BLACK SCARFACE II	$15.00	_____
BLACK SCARFACE III	$15.00	_____
BLACK SCARFACE IV	$15.00	_____
BLACK SCARFACE V	$18.00	_____
DOC	$15.00	_____
KING	$15.00	_____
KING 2	$15.00	_____
THE DYNASTY EMPIRE I	$15.00	_____
THE DYNASTY EMPIRE II	$15.00	_____
KILLADELPHIA	$15.00	_____
ON EVERYTHING I LOVE	$15.00	_____
MONEY DESIRES & REGRETS	$15.00	_____
WHAT EVERY WOMAN WANTS	$15.00	_____
YOUNG RICH & DANGEROUS	$15.00	_____
THE UNDERWORLD	$15.00	_____
A ROSE AMONG THORNS	$15.00	_____
A ROSE AMONG THORNS II	$15.00	_____
SEX SLAVE	$15.00	_____
AIN'T NO SUNSHINE	$15.00	_____
WHO	$15.00	_____
THE DARKEST CORNER	$15.00	_____
HOTTEST SUMMER EVER	$15.00	_____
BLACK GOTTI	$15.00	_____
CONTRACT KILLER	$15.00	_____
THE 21 LESSONS OF LIFE	$12.99	_____
THE 21 LESSONS OF SUCCESS	$12.99	_____
LEGEND	$12.99	_____
SOSA	$15.00	_____
PLEASE DON'T TOUCH ME THERE	$12.99	_____

Please visit www.dasaintentertainment.com to place online orders.

WE SHIP TO PRISONS

Fill out this form and send it
to:
DASAINT ENTERTAINMENT
PO BOX 97
BALA CYNWYD, PA 19004

Make Money Orders payable to:
DASAINT ENTERTAINMENT (NO CHECKS ACCEPTED)

NAME: _____

ADDRESS: _____
_____

CITY: _____ STATE: _____ ZIP: _____

PHONE: _____ EMAIL: _____

PRISON ID NUMBER_____

$4.00 per item for Shipping and Handling
($8.00 per item for Expedited Shipping)

Please visit www.dasaintentertainment.com to place online orders.

WE SHIP TO PRISONS

DUPLICATE FORM

Fill out this form and send it to:
DASAINT ENTERTAINMENT
PO BOX 97
BALA CYNWYD, PA 19004

TITLE	PRICE	QTY
BLACK SCARFACE	$15.00	____
BLACK SCARFACE II	$15.00	____
BLACK SCARFACE III	$15.00	____
BLACK SCARFACE IV	$15.00	____
BLACK SCARFACE V	$18.00	____
DOC	$15.00	____
KING	$15.00	____
KING 2	$15.00	____
THE DYNASTY EMPIRE I	$15.00	____
THE DYNASTY EMPIRE II	$15.00	____
KILLADELPHIA	$15.00	____
ON EVERYTHING I LOVE	$15.00	____
MONEY DESIRES & REGRETS	$15.00	____
WHAT EVERY WOMAN WANTS	$15.00	____
YOUNG RICH & DANGEROUS	$15.00	____
THE UNDERWORLD	$15.00	____
A ROSE AMONG THORNS	$15.00	____
A ROSE AMONG THORNS II	$15.00	____
SEX SLAVE	$15.00	____
AIN'T NO SUNSHINE	$15.00	____
WHO	$15.00	____
THE DARKEST CORNER	$15.00	____
HOTTEST SUMMER EVER	$15.00	____
BLACK GOTTI	$15.00	____
CONTRACT KILLER	$15.00	____
THE 21 LESSONS OF LIFE	$12.99	____
THE 21 LESSONS OF SUCCESS	$12.99	____
LEGEND	$12.99	____
SOSA	$15.00	____
PLEASE DON'T TOUCH ME THERE	$12.99	____

Please visit www.dasaintentertainment.com to place online orders.

WE SHIP TO PRISONS

DUPLICATE FORM

Fill out this form and send it to:
DASAINT ENTERTAINMENT
PO BOX 97
BALA CYNWYD, PA 19004

Make Money Orders Payable To:
DASAINT ENTERTAINMENT (NO CHECKS ACCEPTED)

NAME: _____

ADDRESS: _____

_____

CITY: _____ STATE: _____ ZIP: _____

PHONE: _____ EMAIL: _____

PRISON ID NUMBER_____

$4.00 per item for Shipping and Handling
($8.00 per item for Expedited Shipping)

Please visit www.dasaintentertainment.com to place online orders.

WE SHIP TO PRISONS

Made in the USA
Monee, IL
28 February 2026

45122656R00105